Boy *Peeling* Fruit

by

Anne Renshaw

This novel is entirely a work of fiction. The names, characters and incidents portrayed in it are the product of the author's imagination. Any resemblance to actual persons, living or dead, or events or localities is entirely coincidental.

Paperback Edition 2021
ISBN 9798700225441

Copyright © Anne Renshaw 2021

Anne Renshaw asserts the moral right to be identified as the author of this work. All rights reserved in all media. No part of this publication may be reproduced, stored in a retrieval system, or transmitted, in any form, or by any means, electronic, mechanical, photocopying, recording or otherwise, without the prior written permission of the author and/or publisher.

THE TOWN OF CARAVAGGIO

1582

Michelangelo Merisi, a twelve-year-old boy, stood outside his grandfather's house. It was a modest home on two floors near Porta Seriola, northeast of the town of Caravaggio in Lombardy, Italy. He held a canvas bag containing his meagre possessions and he shifted from one foot to the other impatient to go. He was angry with himself for crying earlier. For appearing weak in front of the men who had dealt with his mother's body. But mostly he was angry with his mother for dying and leaving him alone. Whenever he allowed himself to think of her, of never seeing her again, a tight knot twisted in his stomach, and pain speared his heart. The funeral director and the local priest had spoken about him in low whispers in the corner of his mother's bedroom as she lay there cold and silent. He was an orphan they'd said, and Michelangelo hadn't liked that word.

He leaned against the wall of the house and looked down the road. Everyone was going about their business as if nothing had happened. Well, it hadn't happened to them. They were oblivious to the pain he was in. Six years ago the bubonic plague had ravaged all of Europe, carried and spread by fleas living on the Black Rat. Ships brought it to Italy and from the cities; the plague leeched its way into the small towns and villages. Caravaggio had been one of those towns. Michelangelo's father and almost the rest of his family had been taken. His mother survived but now she was gone too. Michelangelo missed his father's stonemasonry workshop in Milan. He could still hear the grinding of the stone, and the chip, chip, chip of a chisel, but only in his head.

An arrangement had been made for him to be apprenticed to a painter, Simone Peterzano, who although Venetian, now resided in Milan. Michelangelo wasn't unhappy at the prospect of learning about the art of drawing and painting and was eager to be on his way. In the distance, he could see a cloud of dust, a carriage on its way to transport him to Milan.

Hours later the carriage turned onto a narrow road and bumped and jerked until it reached the entrance to Porta Orientale, in the parish of Santa Babila. Michelangelo jumped down and waved goodbye to the man who had driven him there. Beside the main door into Peterzano's home, a metal bell was fixed to the stone surround and Michelangelo tugged at the loop of rope. Within a few minutes, the door creaked inwards and a plump lady stood before him.

'Ah, you must be the young Merisi,' she said, beckoning him over the threshold. 'Come, my husband is expecting you.'

Michelangelo followed Signora Angelica Peterzano along a passage and up a stone staircase. She opened the door into a wide tall ceilinged room and gave him a push propelling him into the room. Michelangelo stood mesmerised. One side of the room was so bright it hurt his eyes. Three tall multi-paned windows embraced the sun and triangles of light glimmered on silver tankards and an array of glazed porcelain dishes placed on a side table. The edges and corners of the room were swathed in shadow. Behind the door he'd just entered, a floor-length red velvet curtain hung, and like blood, the surplus cloth pooled on the floor. The scene imprinted itself into his memory, to be duplicated many times in his paintings years later.

Michelangelo noticed his tutor watching him. The painter stood back from a tall easel, palette in hand as if he'd been scrutinising his work so far, and then noticed the new arrival.

'Caravaggio, come here and let me look at you.' Peterzano said.

'My name is Michelangelo Merisi, Signor.' The boy held his head high, an arrogant stance even at his young age.

'Yes I know, but I will call you Caravaggio.' Peterzano smiled reassuringly. He had heard promising rumours about the Merisi boy, and so when approached by his uncle, readily agreed to become his tutor.

Michelangelo, re Caravaggio, lived within the home of Peterzano's family but it wasn't until he was thirteen years old that a contract of apprenticeship was signed. It bound Caravaggio to Peterzano for a further four years and during this time he was instructed on every aspect of art. He studied anatomy and perspective, learned how to prepare the oils and mix colour. To practice his art, Caravaggio liked to use models and he sketched and painted numerous versions of the same subject. A young boy, also to eventually become a student, worked in Peterzano's kitchen and was one such subject. Caravaggio produced numerous paintings of the boy peeling fruit, combining his skills in portrait and still life.

Caravaggio: Boy Peeling Fruit
Public domain, via Wikimedia Commons

THE CHURCH of SAL CELSO, MILAN

1924

The small boy lay fully clothed in his bed waiting for the signal. He didn't know the time, or when the signal would come, but that didn't matter. It was dark outside and his parents and siblings were all in their beds asleep. They knew nothing of the secret mission he and his uncle had arranged.

The sound came to him a short while later, a scattering of pebbles on his window, and the boy left the warm cocoon of his blankets. He descended the wooden stairs careful not to make a sound. His Uncle, Riccardo, waited for him in the narrow street and without a word they walked quickly towards their destination, making sure to keep to the shadows.

They soon reached the old church of Sal Celso. His uncle led the way around to the side of the building and the boy followed. It was dark there with thick bushes and dense hawthorn hiding them from view should anyone pass by on the road. His uncle pointed to a broken stained glass window halfway up the church wall. The open space was just big enough for a small boy to climb through. His uncle hoisted the boy up and pushed him in.

The ground was further away than the boy expected and he landed heavily on the stone floor. Luckily the area underneath the window was clear and he stood up uninjured. He took a small torch out of his pocket and flicked it on. Everywhere had a layer of dust and the cool evening breeze coming through the break in the window quivered cobwebs hanging from an overhead beam. The narrow beam of light picked out wooden pews, a pile of discarded prayer books, and a stack of paintings in gilded frames propped up against a wall. The paintings were what interested his uncle. That was why they were here. Nothing else mattered. The boy shone his torch and jumped in fright when he saw the face of another boy. He stood staring at the boy for a moment and then heard his uncle's voice call to him from outside.

'Have you found anything?'

'Yes, but all the paintings are in large frames and too heavy for me to lift.' The boy heard a rough scrape and scrambling from outside and suddenly his uncle's head appeared in the break in the glass.

'Leave them for now. Go and look in the corners and up by the lectern. Hurry up.' The boy did as he was told and found another four paintings, not in frames but rolled and tied with string. He gathered them up and rushed back to the window.

'Uncle, I've found them, help me up.' The boy waited. He wasn't worried when his uncle didn't answer straight away. He's probably gone for a pee, he thought. He didn't have to wait long before he heard a voice outside and a few minutes later a head appeared at the window again. The boy sighed with relief and passed the rolls of canvas one by one, placing them into the man's outstretched hand. The man didn't speak, and as soon as he had the paintings in his hand his face disappeared from the window.

'Uncle, are you still there?' The boy called, but again no reply came. He squatted underneath the window waiting to be lifted up and out of the gloomy church. While he waited he looked again at the boy in the painting and then took out his pocket knife and cut the canvas away from the frame.

Later, as the dawn light filtered through the stained

glass windows the boy woke and he could see more clearly his surroundings. It took him all his strength to pull the nearest pew towards the broken window. Hunger, thirst and cold had weakened him, but it spurred him on and he heaved the pew up on its end against the wall. Carefully, using the pew like a ladder and with the painting tucked under his arm, he scrambled up the wooden pew and climbed out of the window.

His uncle sat a few yards away, his back up against the outside church wall, his legs splayed at a strange angle. The boy crouched down beside him and gave his sleeve a pull. His uncle's head lolled towards him and vacant glassy eyes glared back at the boy. Startled and upset the boy raced home. He hoped he would make it back into his bed before anyone in the house noticed he had been out.

The small boy's uncle, Riccardo Cortez, was found a few days later. His family buried him in the quiet cemetery near the church. Nothing came of the investigation into his death.

A few weeks' later two art historians and researchers cleared Sal Celso church. They took everything they found to Sforzesco Castle, in Milan, where they were stored, again hidden from sight, until 2012.

LONDON BRIDGE HOSPITAL – CITY OF LONDON

SPRING 2019

Julie Merriton walked away from the oncologist's department out of the hospital and into the fresh air. Air, according to her consultant she wouldn't be enjoying for very much longer. Nine months he told her, after his diagnosis of end-stage colon cancer. It had spread to her liver, not yet her lungs, and he'd gone on to explain the treatment on offer. She'd known for months that something wasn't right, but at fifty-eight years old she had never envisaged this. Julie was surprised she hadn't broken down in tears as she'd sat in the room listening to the prognosis, a nurse on hand by her side ready with tissues. Shock, disbelief, or plain acceptance, she knew her tears wouldn't change anything.

Robotically Julie drove away from the hospital. Her dead mother's words sounded softly in her ear, "everything happens in three's." Well, that was what her mother believed, and now perhaps Julie did too. Everything in her life was falling apart, and she mentally counted, proving her mother right.

Her Art and Antique store in London was struggling after she'd made a few too many misguided purchases. Her partner of five years, Matthew, happened to mention during dinner a week ago that he had fallen in love with someone else. He'd reminded her that as it was his house they shared, Julie should look for somewhere else to live. If not she would be homeless at the end of the month.

Not strictly true though. She had kept hold of her apartment in Chester, despite Matthew's earlier insistence she should sell it. He'd encouraged her to move to London to live with him, and then to use the money from the sale to take advantage of the bigger and better opportunities there. Thank goodness she'd ignored his advice. Her Chester apartment, adjacent to Grosvenor Park and in a prestigious development had gone up considerably in value. A splendid location and Julie knew when the time came it wouldn't be difficult to sell. It seemed that time was now imminent. The third happening, her cancer, made the other two seem insignificant now.

Julie parked her car and sat for a few minutes deciding whether she should tell Matthew her news. Would he be sympathetic, probably not? Did she want his pity, definitely not?

There was so much she still wanted to do with her life, and nine months was too short a time to do it all in. It was enough time for her to put her affairs in order, though, and that's what Julie intended to do.

CHAPTER 1

Mark and Vivien Anderson shared their home, Lilac House, with Isobel their eighteen-year-old daughter. Their business, Anderson Antiques, ran from a converted barn that stood a good distance away from the house and on the outskirts of Woodbury. A gravelled car park, enough for several customers' vehicles filled up the space between the barn and the boundary. On entering the building the first thing that hit you was the smell. Beeswax on oak polished a hundred times, the mustiness of parchment, oil on canvas, Persian rugs and vintage fabrics. The barn was mezzanine with a broad staircase leading to the upper floor. Oil paintings mostly but watercolours too filled every space on the walls up there. Except for the occasional narrow area housing Grandfather clocks, whose continuous loud tick-tock filled the silence of the building when empty?

Mark's friend, David Lanceley, Woodbury's previous vicar had recently returned from a business trip to Italy, and while he and Mark were having drinks in the local pub, Mark mentioned his intention of booking a summer holiday. As soon as Mark said, holiday, David recommended Rome. Mark listened with interest while David enthused in particular about Piazza Navona.

'It's situated in the heart of Rome's historic district and one of Rome's most beautiful piazzas. A fountain supports an Egyptian obelisk, and although it's known for its unique 17^{th}century Baroque appearance, with its ornate buildings, churches and museums, there are also numerous shops, cafés and bars.' Mark listened twisting his empty glass in his hand as David continued. 'I managed to do a little sightseeing while I was there, but not enough. I've booked to go again in June, a proper holiday this time. If you do go, Galleria Borghese is a must for you to visit, Mark. It holds the private collection of the Borghese family and is open to the public. Old master paintings such as Titian's Sacred and Profane Love, dating from 1514 is displayed there.'

David didn't need to say anymore. Mark's passion for renaissance paintings had him hooked and he was already there in his head, but David went on.

'Vivien would love the Trevi Fountain and the Piazza di Spagna is so romantic. Everywhere is easy to get to and the hotel I stay in provides coaches and a tour guide.' David took a breath and a long swallow of his beer then stood. 'Got time for another?' he asked.

'Cheers,' Mark raised his glass.

Later that day, Mark checked prices and availability at Travel Agents online. He didn't mention it to his wife, Vivien, but he'd made a decision. He was going to Rome.

In May, a few weeks before his trip to Rome, out of the blue a woman Mark hadn't heard from in several years, telephoned and left a message urging him to ring her as soon as he could, and he wondered what had precipitated the call. Intrigued, he rang the number she had left. Julie answered almost immediately.

'Mark, how are you these days?'

The sound of Julie Merriton's sultry voice brought back memories Mark was reluctant to revisit.

He'd first met Julie in his early days of trying his hand in the antique buying and selling business. She was the older woman, glamorous and sophisticated, then in her late thirties, he a twenty-three-year-old, and the age difference hadn't mattered. To begin with, he was flattered and grateful. Julie introduced him to other antique dealers, auctioneers and influential buyers. In her spacious sumptuous apartment above her antique shop, Julie's sexual desires and endless energy had elated him. He became attached to her, serious, naively thinking she reciprocated his feelings of love. For Julie, he had been a distraction, an ego boost to her loss of self-esteem after a long and messy divorce. Gradually she began to distance herself, and it wasn't long before he'd been replaced by someone new.

'What do you want, Julie?' Mark asked flatly.

'Oh, don't be like that Mark. I've moved back to Chester and thought I would look you up. Can you manage to get away from your business for a couple of hours tomorrow?'

'I repeat, what do you want?' Mark regretted ringing her and was in two minds whether to replace the receiver, but he knew Julie wouldn't be satisfied until she'd said her piece. He heard her sigh.

'As I said, I'm back in Chester again, but while living in London I acquired several useful contacts, also in Europe. I'm willing to pass their information on to you if you're interested. Look, Mark, can we let bygones be just that? Will you meet me tomorrow? I've booked a table at the Grosvenor Hotel for one o'clock, and I hope you can make it.'

The Grosvenor Hotel's ground floor restaurant was crowded and from where Mark sat he had a good view through the window of the ornate Chester Clock, placed above the bridge that crossed over the road. A group of Japanese tourists' craned their necks to look up at it and take in the intricacy of its design.

White table cloths smoothed over small square tables

dotted the space and customers sat elbow to elbow in unwanted intimacy. Julie waved a waiter over who squeezed towards them to take their order. She settled on a smoked salmon salad and ordered it for them both. Once the waiter had gone she placed her hand on Mark's arm to bring his attention away from the window and back to her.

'Are you still obsessed with Caravaggio?' she asked.' Mark's answer was a Gallic shrug. 'If you are then I think you'll be interested in what I have to tell you.' Julie spoke quietly as though not wanting anyone else to hear. 'We'll get to that later, let's eat first.'

Throughout the meal Julie made light conversation talking mainly about her, avoiding the only subject Mark was now interested in. He noticed that she had lost a lot of weight, that it was unflattering. He watched her animated gestures with amusement and looking at her now, he couldn't quite believe he had ever loved her. He realised it had been infatuation. Julie's natural auburn hair wasn't natural anymore and her large brown eyes outlined in kohl, as they had been all those years ago, no longer enticed him. She had always dressed conservatively, her clothes noticeably expensive, sometimes provocative, but never flamboyant. Today, Mark found her too big long flowery dress gaudy.

Julie noticed Mark observing her from across the table. 'Mark darling enough about me, how are you? Have you really settled down to country life?'

'Yes, and you know I'm married now, Julie.'

'I heard. What her name?' Julie asked trying to sound interested.

'Vivien and we have an eighteen-year-old daughter, Isobel.' Mark said proudly. 'My antique business is doing extremely well actually, and the collection of old masters I've acquired over the years have steadily increased in value. Mark leaned back and raised his wine glass. He clicked the glass to hers, his expression smug.

'Admirable,' Julie said, somewhat sarcastically. 'Have you obtained the elusive Caravaggio yet?'

Mark shook his head. 'No, and it's unlikely I ever will.'

'Don't be too sure, what if I told you, a painting by Caravaggio has been offered to me to purchase.'

'A forgery then?' Mark snorted in derision.

'Not necessarily.'

'I'm listening.' Mark leaned forward eager to hear what Julie had to say.

'First, do you know who Caravaggio was apprenticed to as a young man?'

'You know I do. Simone Peterzano, a mannerist painter, who lived in Milan.'

'Correct. What do you think happened to all those early sketches and paintings his students, including Caravaggio, did while being tutored by him?' Julie asked, still keeping her voice low.

'You're on about the discovery in Castello Sforzesco, in Milan. That was in 2012, and if I remember correctly, although they found remarkable similarities I haven't heard any were authenticated as Caravaggio's work. The drawings and sketches will have little if any artistic importance, so worthless unless signed.'

'I agree about the sketches, probably his students' exercises, but many were found to be preliminary drawings of work that Caravaggio went on to paint. The paintings by Peterzano and the drawings by some of the young artists tutored by him are signed and although they're a significant part of the find, they're not considered as important as Caravaggio's work. Curators from the Galleria Degli Uffizi in Florence visited Castello Sforzesco to assess the findings. There was a lot of scepticism at the time, and negative media coverage didn't help but at last, every item discovered has been documented and arrangements have been made for the collection to be taken to Rome.'

'So?' Mark eyed Julie wondering where all this was leading.

'Well, through my contacts, I've recently learned that one of the paintings was stolen. He assured me it is from the selection considered to be by Caravaggio.'

'Let me ask you a question. Is it signed?'

Julie glanced around her again before continuing. 'Caravaggio only ever signed one painting, The Beheading of John the Baptist, as you well know. That fact is what has caused all the controversy. The finds attributed to him are not signed, so no, there's no proof they were drawn or painted by him. The painting on offer isn't signed either but that doesn't mean it isn't a genuine Caravaggio.'

'Stolen before being authenticated then, so I doubt it is, and I must say I'm surprised you've been taken in.'

'During the last year of his apprenticeship, striving for perfection, Caravaggio painted several versions of the same subject. Boy Peeling Fruit, oil on canvas, was one of them. By 1592 he had attained the precision he craved and went on to the paint, Boy with Basket of Fruit.' Julie took a sip of wine and waited for Mark's response.

'Are you saying that the painting on offer is an early version of Boy Peeling Fruit?'

'Yes, I am. The size of the painting is sixty-three by sixty-three centimetres, or thereabouts, and is small in comparison to his later work, but the size adds to its credibility.'

'Hmmm fascinating, Julie, but I don't understand why you're telling me about it. Surely you're interested in acquiring the painting for yourself?' Mark hailed a waiter. 'Whiskey straight,' he ordered.

Julie grinned at him. 'Needing something to calm your nerves?'

'Sod off.' Mark sneered.

'I'm offering you a temporary partnership.' Julie told him. 'An Italian entrepreneur owns it and has let it known to the right people that it's for sale. The painting could have been stolen to order for all I know, but I don't care, Mark.'

Mark had taken a sip of whisky and nearly choked. 'We're not talking Mafia here are we?'

'Have you ever watched the film, The Thomas Crown Affair?'

'I think I may have, so what?'

'It's about art theft and insurance fraud and has nothing to do with any Cartel or Mafia, so let's not let our imagination run away with us. Anyway, as I was about to tell you, the owner is demanding the payment be made in uncut diamonds, and that's where you come in. You're going to Rome soon, aren't you?' Julie sat back, and looked at Mark on tenterhooks, hopeful he would take the bait.

'How do you know I'm going to Rome?'

'Someone mentioned it to me, I can't remember who.'

'Why raw diamonds, I don't understand.' Mark asked, deciding to go along with her for the time being.

'They're cheaper to obtain actually. The diamonds are to be taken to a jeweller in Rome, but he is just a go-between. Delivering uncut diamonds to a jeweller is normal and legitimate, and using a third party is a way of preventing a paper trail.

He will pay for the diamonds in Euros. Once you have the Euros from him, you pay the owner for the painting.'

Mark had a thought. 'If I'm getting the Caravaggio, how do you benefit from this?'

'If you must know I'm in debt to the owner. I bought an item of his at Sotheby's, paid over the odds actually and I haven't been able to sell it on and recuperate any profit. He accepted a part payment at the time, but I still owe him fifty thousand in sterling. He's now insisting I pay the balance before the end of June, and wants the transaction done this way. He wants to offload the painting, get it out of the country I think, so he asked if I knew anyone who might be interested. He wants two hundred thousand pounds for the painting, also paid in rough diamonds. Alonzo and I go back a long way. He gave me first refusal but I can't raise that amount at such short notice, Mark, and that's when I thought of you. I know how much owning a Caravaggio would mean to you.'

'You want me to give you two hundred thousand pounds for a stolen painting that in all probability hasn't been painted by Caravaggio. Give me a break, Julie. In any case, why should I take all the risks? Supposing I'm searched at the airport, isn't it illegal to carry uncut diamonds out of the UK and into another country?'

'We're still within the EU at the moment; otherwise, there could be a problem. I've checked the Kimberley Process certification scheme and the paperwork for the diamonds will all be in order before you leave.'

'How will you obtain the diamonds, that won't be easy?'

Julie shifted in her seat. 'You don't need to worry about that as I said, I have contacts in Europe.

'This could be a swindle. Have you thought of that?'

'Take a few days to think it over, but let me know as soon as. The diamonds have to be delivered to an address in Rome before the end of June. If you agree, my contact will make him-self known to you after you arrive and give you the jewellers address. This is an opportunity of a lifetime for you. It's what you always dreamed of, isn't it? Just imagine what a Caravaggio painting will be worth in five or ten years.' When Mark didn't reply Julie went on. 'I have to give them my answer before the end of next week, so if you're in, you'll need to get the money to me quickly so I can acquire the additional diamonds.' Julie applied lipstick and stood. 'Don't worry about the bill, I'll see to it.' She placed a kiss on Mark's cheek and walked away.

Mark wiped away her kiss with his serviette and downed the rest of his whiskey.

Over the next few days, Mark considered what Julie had suggested. He had clients who were chomping at the bit to get their hands on some of the paintings he had on display in the barn but not as yet for sale, so he could raise the money if he put his mind to it. Although not as quickly as Julie required. Nevertheless, he telephoned her and agreed. Mark also contemplated what David had said about Vivien accompanying him to Rome. He'd immediately dismissed it at the time. Having his wife tagging along with him wasn't Mark's idea of a holiday. Now he reconsidered. Perhaps Vivien wouldn't be a hindrance, she could come in very useful after all.

On Friday, a few days after his meeting with Julie, Mark met David in the Royal Oak Pub. It was a weekly tradition, their men's night out. Mark waited until David had come back with the drinks and had sat down before he asked. 'David, how are your investments these days?'

'Doing quite well, I'm pleased to say. I doubted my sister's judgment you know when she asked me to loan her money to invest, but she came up trumps, and I've certainly benefitted by listening to her.'

'How is Leonie?' Mark wasn't interested in David's sister but thought it polite to ask.

'I don't see much of her but she's well enough.'

'David, look, I hate to ask you this, but could you loan me a hundred thousand pounds? I need it quickly and there isn't time to go through my bank.' Mark failed to mention he was already in the process of securing a loan at his bank for the other hundred thousand that he needed. 'I've been approached regarding a great investment but I don't have all the ready cash. I'll be able to pay you back in full in a few months. It's really important to me otherwise I wouldn't ask.'

David noticed Mark's hand shaking as he picked up his beer to take a swallow. 'Phew, a hundred thousand, that's a lot of money Mark. Is the investment in property, like mine?'

'Yes, sort of, and the thought of missing this opportunity is giving me sleepless nights.'

'You'll need to tell me more about it before I part with my cash.'

'I can't David. It's a matter of trust. Will you help me?'

David didn't say anything for a while. He sat sipping his beer and when he'd finished it, he said. 'It's your round.'

Mark picked up the empty glasses and went to the bar. He glanced over his shoulder at David a few times while waiting to be served, hoping he was considering his request.

David made a quick call on his mobile, and when he noticed Mark looking at him he put his thumb up in an okay signal. Mark returned to the table and placed a beer and a whisky chaser down in front of David.

'I don't need bribery,' David said, indicating the whisky. 'I've just been on the telephone to my financial advisor. His advice is that before I agree to loan you that amount of money, I should have some sort of surety.'

'What kind of surety,' Mark asked.

'A twenty-five per cent share of Anderson Antiques seems fair to me.'

'You want a quarter of my business, that's a bit steep.'

'It's Vivien's business too, isn't it? She owns half, so you'll probably want to talk to her about it first. We'll have to go through my solicitors to have the legal agreement drawn up, and I would expect you to pay the costs for that. Once that's sorted, I'll have the money available for you. In any case, if you pay me back within a few months as promised, the agreement can be made void. You'll have your investment and your original half share of the business.'

'You drive a hard bargain, but I agree, and we don't need to worry Vivien. Let's keep this between ourselves.'

CHAPTER 2

The temperature had been 23 degrees Celsius when Mark and Vivien left Manchester airport, a sunny day with not a cloud in the sky, only to arrive in Rome during a sudden downpour and dark clouds. Rain splattered the coach windows and sapped Vivien's enthusiasm as she looked out onto smudged buildings; empty outdoor café tables and wet pavements.

When David told her Mark had booked a holiday to Rome she never imagined she was included. Mark regularly travelled around the British countryside on his own looking for old paintings and objet d'art to sell in the barn. He'd never asked her to accompany him on one of his jaunts.

Vivien first met Mark at an antique fair in Chester. She had just moved into her first property, a small two bedroomed terraced house in Christleton, a suburb of Chester. All she owned other than the house was a bed, the necessary white goods, and basics, and she'd gone to the fair on the lookout for inexpensive items to make the house a home. After strolling up and down the stalls scrutinising every table filled with collectables and doubtful antiques, her eyes alighted on an oil painting. A copy in the style of Vermeer's, View of Delft. Mark had it priced for ninety pounds, and Vivien cleverly bartered him down to sixty. During the five minutes it took to haggle, she was smitten. 'Make it fifty-five pounds and I'll buy you a coffee,' she said, holding out her hand for him to shake.

Mark took her hand and replied, 'Done, providing you let me buy you dinner tonight.'

Nine months later they married. Mark was everything Vivien had dreamed of in a husband and they both settled into a state of marital bliss. With the housing market stable, they decided to put the equity from the sale of Vivien's house and Mark's canal-side apartment down as a substantial deposit on a four bedroomed farmhouse with five acres of land, in Woodbury. After selling off a large portion of the land to an adjacent farmer, a lot of hard work and costly renovations, Lilac House, set in a quarter of an acre of landscaped gardens, became their dream home. They then set about renovating the large barn now empty of livestock. This was where they intended to run their Antique business, and after more hard work it soon turned from a smelly cowshed into a welcoming space. The business had been Mark's idea and a successful one.

Had it not been for Isobel, born three years after their marriage, everything would have carried on the same. At least, that was what Vivien thought. Instead, Mark became bitter about the time she needed to spend with the baby and the resulting extra work he'd ended up overloaded with. He began going out every evening and come home aggressive, fuelled with alcohol. It started with a slap to Vivien's face if Isobel was fractious and wouldn't settle. The slap became a punch. Vivien tolerated the verbal and physical abuse blaming herself for her inadequacy as a mother.

The coach pulled to a stop outside Hotel Muscatello, the one recommended by David. The rain had stopped and the wet pavements had dried under the hot sun. Vivien gathered up their belongings while Mark made sure he was first off the coach to reclaim their suitcases.

Nervy wasn't Mark's thing and it was out of character for him to rush but he wouldn't relax until he had taken the diamonds out of Vivien's suitcase. Vivien had proved useful for once and had waltzed through the airport check-in and security without causing a blink. Not that there was anything to worry about. Julie had assured him that all the paperwork was in order, and the forms were tucked away safely in the inside pocket of his jacket. Mark waited to one side of the coach for his wife and when Vivien stepped off the coach he waved. Although his love for Vivien had waned years ago he looked at her approvingly. She was still quite attractive, in her way. She used little makeup and never wore to excess the latest fashion. It was what had drawn him to her in the first place, that and her love of antiques. He wondered why she'd stayed with him all these years and had a fleeting moment of guilt.

The hotel's roof terrace restaurant had panoramic views of Rome from the Dome of St. Peter to the Pantheon, but the following morning due to the inclement weather, David Lanceley, who had arrived a few days earlier, decided to breakfast in the restaurant on the first floor. While waiting for his breakfast to be served he glanced across the room to where Vivien Anderson sat, grateful that she still valued him as one of her best friends. Even though he'd had no right to be jealous, it had knocked him for six when she'd married Mark. Now his romantic state of mind and the affection he still harboured for her had to be kept on hold.

Mark watched his wife pick at her breakfast while he tucked into his with relish. 'Is there a problem?' he queried.

'No it's fine, I'm not hungry.' Vivien pushed scrambled eggs to one side of her plate.

'There's no pleasing you, is there? I've paid good money for this holiday; the least you could do is show some appreciation. Just eat it, and don't make such a fuss.'

Dutifully Vivien scrapped the egg onto her fork and put it in her mouth. Mark watched her with satisfaction. He noticed Vivien wasn't wearing her hair in its usual style. Today it hung long and limp shadowing each side of her face. He guessed why. 'You look like a ferret with your hair down, did you know that,' he told her spitefully.

Vivien put down her fork and smoothed her hair behind her ears letting Mark see the bruising he'd caused. She couldn't remember what she had done to set him off the previous evening. Maybe she'd forgotten to pack something he needed. She remembered him shouting something about a blue shirt just before his fist swung into her face. She felt tears well up and pretended to blow her nose so that she could wipe them away before Mark noticed. After a few minutes, ashamed that she allowed this to happen and not wanting other breakfasting guests to see the bruises, she shook her hair loose again.

'You shouldn't provoke me, Vivien. You know how it will end if you cross me.' Mark hailed a waiter for more coffee and then picked up his newspaper. He lifted it to his face blocking out Vivien from his view.

Vivien spread butter onto a piece of toast and lifted it to her mouth. The sleeve of her blouse slipped to her elbow revealing more bruises and she lowered her arm.

Vivien glanced at the newspaper. She could just see Mark's hair peeping above its pages. Suddenly he lowered the newspaper making her visibly jump.

'Well, I'll be dammed. Look at this.' Mark whipped the paper round and laid it across the table, covering everything including Vivien's toast.

Mark's finger jabbed at an article, and as Vivien read the headline she understood his excitement. Mark chuckled to himself. This confirmed everything Julie had said, and he wondered if she'd known that the artwork found in Castello Sforzesco was scheduled to be on display while he was in Rome. He looked across the tables to where David Lanceley sat, then stood and waved the paper. 'David, have you got a minute. I want to show you something.' Mark shouted above the hum of the other guests.

David waved back in acknowledgement. He didn't rush instead he finished off his coffee, folded his napkin neatly, and then strolled across the restaurant to where they sat. He stood beside Vivien facing Mark.

Mark showed him the article. 'Look at this.'

David read part of it out loud. 'A collection of paintings and drawings found in a church in Milan were transferred to the original workshop of Peterzano in Milan.'

Mark interrupted him. 'To be precise, nearly fourteen hundred works in Simone Peterzano's archive were scattered between several churches in Milan and were discovered in Castello Sforzesco in 2012. They include paintings and drawings by Peterzano and the young artists who were tutored by him. Did you know that Michelangelo Merisi, known as Caravaggio, was one of those young artists? Some of the paintings are believed to date from Caravaggio's apprenticed years. Isn't it amazing?'

Intrigued, David carried on reading the full article. 'It says here that if the sketches and paintings prove to be authentic their estimated value would be worth seven hundred million euro. That's nearly six hundred million pounds, sterling.' David looked at Mark sceptically. 'It could be another art scam you know. If they were found in 2012, why has it taken so long for them to come to

Rome?'

'Who cares? Anyway, I thought I'd go to the Palazzo Doria Pamphilj this morning and try and find out more. Come with me, we can form our own opinion.'

Vivien knew the love of Mark's life was art, particularly Caravaggio's work. No Picasso or Van Goff could ever get him this excited, and the expression on Mark's face confirmed it. Uncharacteristically his eyes shone with joy.

'Sorry Mark, I've already made plans for this morning.' David stated.

'Can't you change them?' David shook his head in answer. Mark looked pointedly at his wife and then stormed off without another word.

David sat down in the vacant seat opposite Vivien. 'Are you all right Viv?'

Vivien flashed him a weak smile. David was the only one who ever called her Viv, and he had done since their days at Christleton Junior School. In their teens, they had "gone out together" which meant they held hands in the cinema and kissed goodnight inside the porch by her front door. She could hardly believe it was more than twenty years ago. She'd always known David would probably follow in his father's and grandfather's footsteps, so it shouldn't have surprised her when he enrolled at Trinity College in Bristol for theological study. But it did. David's lack of commitment finally made sense. When he eventually became the Vicar of St. Martins Church in Woodbury, they had rekindled their friendship, albeit a platonic one. Then a few years ago, much to everyone's surprise, David had shed his dog collar along with his religious calling. He'd moved out of the vicarage, taking his cat Fidget with him, and bought a three bedroomed detached house on a new housing estate in Lower Shelton. His faith now rested on the value of his property investments in the U.K, and overseas.

David leaned over and took Vivien's hand in his. 'He hasn't hurt you again has he?' Vivien smiled and fiddled with her hair ignoring the question. 'I'm going to do some gift shopping this morning before the tour. Would you come with me? I need ideas on what to buy for Leonie?'

'A leather handbag roomy enough for all her stuff would be my suggestion,' Vivien told him.

'Will you come and help me to choose one.' David insisted, but Vivien declined the offer. Impulsively he made another suggestion. 'Alright, so how about we have an early lunch together on the roof terrace when I return?'

'Thank you, but I'd better not.' Vivien heard Mark's voice in her head and was dismayed by how cowed she'd become.

'Sorry, I'm not taking no for an answer,' David replied firmly. 'Mark can join us if he's back by then. Don't let me down, Viv.' David's warm smile cheered Vivien and she found herself agreeing. Surely Mark wouldn't object to her having lunch with an old friend.

Mark watched the floor numbers light up as the elevator descended from their third-floor room. The doors shuddered open on the ground floor and Mark walked towards the exit. Halfway across the foyer, he stopped. Their tour guide, Helena Cortez, leaned against the reception desk. She noticed him and smiled, and gave a little wave. As always with the female sex Mark felt the need to impress and self-assured he strolled to where she stood. Helena wore her long dark hair in a loose chignon. Wispy strands hung beside her cheeks and softened her strong features. Her uniform jacket was an unflattering dark navy but she'd added elegance by draping a chiffon scarf around her neck.

Also at the desk, a young man stood talking to one of the male receptionists. He turned as Mark approached and took his place beside Helena. 'Mark, let me introduce you to my brother, Antonio.' Helena linked arms with her brother and rested her head on his shoulder affectionately.

Mark took in the man's clear olive skin, black shoulder-length wavy hair, and pale hazel eyes with a pang of jealousy. 'Bon journo,' Mark said and offered his hand.

Antonio obliged with a half-hearted handshake. 'I believe we have a mutual friend.'

'Have we?' Mark replied cautiously.

'Julie Merriton, a business colleague. Although I believe your relationship with her wasn't all business.' Antonio smiled and winked at him.

'How dare she, my private life isn't any of your business.' Mark blustered, affronted by the man's insolence.

Antonio shrugged and began to move away, his face a blank mask.

Helena placed her hand on Antonio's arm. 'Please don't go yet.' she said, 'and remember, Mark is a guest in the hotel, show some respect.'

Antonio kissed his sister lightly on the cheek and gave Mark an apologetic look. 'I'll see you later, Helena,' he said, walking away.

'Take no notice of him Mark. Anyway, are you coming on the tour this afternoon? The coach leaves at one o'clock sharp.'

Mark assured her that he'd be there and then headed outside. Antonio was waiting for him. Mark ignored him and hailed a taxi.

'I'm sorry we got off to a bad start, Mr Anderson, but I do need to speak to you. My car is parked nearby. Let me drive you to your destination and we can chat on the way. Where do you want to go?' Antonio said.

Mark had attempted to flag down two more taxis while Antonio spoke but the drivers had ignored him and raced past. He only had a couple of hours to get to the museum and back and hopefully have time for a quick lunch, so he agreed to let Antonio take him.

'Palazzo Doria Pamphilj,' Mark said and followed Antonio into a side street where the young man's Fiat Panda was parked. Antonio manoeuvred the car out of the narrow street and then sped along Via del Sediari weaving through honking horns and noisy scooters.

Coming straight to the point Antonio said, 'I presume you had no trouble going through Customs?'

'No, why would I.' Mark snapped.

'Julie gave you a package of uncut diamonds to bring with you to Rome.'

'I have no idea what you are talking about.'

'Mr Anderson, I'm the contact Julie told you about. You can trust me. You have Julie's mobile number, don't you? Check with her and she will confirm it. I'll tell you all you need to know later. Please make sure no one else knows your main reason for visiting Rome.'

'My reason for being here is to have a relaxing holiday.' Mark replied, silently fuming. Julie hadn't given him her mobile number. Her landline was his only means of communicating with her, and he was determined to do just that as soon as he returned to the hotel.

Antonio was silent for the rest of the journey and dropped Mark off in Via del Corso a few yards from the entrance to the museum.

Mark bought a ticket into the museum and then spoke to an official-looking gentleman standing by the entrance.

'I came here hoping to see these,' Mark shoved the

English newspaper under the man's nose. 'Which part of the building are they in?'

The man answered in rapid-fire Italian accompanied by hand gestures and much shaking of his head. Mark didn't have to be fluent in the language to know that the artwork he was there to see hadn't been put on display yet. Disappointed Mark wandered into the main gallery. Above him, high ceilings depicted a multitude of cherubs and the elaborately carved beams were white and gold. He counted seven arched stain glass windows along each side of the walls and in-between each window huge mirrors in ornate gold frames reflected the light. In front of each mirror on a marble plinth statues were placed, each different in their pose. From the ceiling hung low chandeliers brightly lit, and the intricate mosaic tiled floor gleamed underneath. Although thrilled by the lavish surroundings, uneasiness spoiled Mark's full enjoyment. All it would take was a telephone call to Julie to confirm Antonio's reliability. But even then, could he trust Julie. Was he being played? Once that thought entered his mind he couldn't get rid of it.

CHAPTER 3

The tour bus left Hotel Muscatello full. Helena sat at the front with the driver and using a microphone she gave snippets of touristy delights they could enjoy while in Rome. The bus dropped them off at Via Della Stamperia, the street leading to the Trevi Fountain. They followed Helena strolling, taking in the atmosphere of their surroundings. The assortment of men and women consisted mainly of middle-aged couples, who like Vivien, preferred sedate meanderings through museums and ancient ruins, rather than the ritual sun-worshipping of their youth. They passed a row of apartments with shops underneath selling either souvenirs or boutique fashion. A low babbling noise drew their attention as they drew nearer to the end of the narrow road. Out of sight excited voices and laughter intermingled with the cascade of water spurred them all on. Vivien could see Mark ahead leading the way with Helena. She watched her husband let his hand caress the young woman's waist, and embarrassed Vivien looked away.

The throng of tourists rounded the corner and suddenly there it was, the Trevi Fountain, huge and overpoweringly glorious. Vivien had read up on its history before her holiday. She knew the fountain had been built in 19 B.C. and was the terminal part of the Vergine aqueduct built by Agrippa, one of Augustus's generals, to bring water from the Salone springs 19 km away, to Rome. The aqueduct still supplied water to the numerous fountains in the historic centre, from Piazza

Navona to Piazza di Spagna.

Vivien hadn't imagined anything so monumental and she gasped in amazement as she walked in a daze towards the semi-circle of stone steps. Men, women and children crowded every corner, some gaping at the fountain's splendour. A party of school children sat in a row along the curved lowest step, the girls in green gingham dresses and straw boaters, the boys in khaki shirts and grey trousers. They made wishes and threw coins in the fountain under the supervision of two adults who sat at either end of the row.

The sun shone unmercifully on everyone. Its rays crystallised the rippling water and stars danced and shimmered in the glare. Finding a clear space Vivien sat down and pulled the brim of her straw hat further over her face. The action wasn't only to protect her face from the sun but to hide the bruises around her right eye. Perspiration trickled her neck and she pulled a handkerchief from her bag and dabbed the moisture away. Looking through the mass of people she spotted her husband standing on the outskirts of the crowd. Even with his back to the fountain, there was no mistaking him. To Vivien, he looked ridiculous in his cream coloured jacket, black cotton shirt and shorts, and his straw trilby tilted at an angle on his head. Helena was with him, her back pressed up against a wall. She'd taken off her uniform jacket and her pale cream sleeveless blouse exposed her clear bronzed skin. Even in the heat, she looked cool and stylish. Vivien couldn't see her husband's face or his expression, but she watched him extend his hand and smooth strands of hair away from Helena's face.

It was just a gentle touch, a seemingly innocent scene, an action a father might make when with his daughter.

Vivien's glance went through and beyond them and she wondered how long it would be before this young woman found him a joke. Vivien tilted her face towards the sun and closed her eyes. She felt the warmth soothe her aches and warm her soul.

Vivien became aware of someone sitting down on the stone step beside her as she felt the brush of cloth on her arm. She opened her eyes and surreptitiously looked to see who it was, warily expecting it to be Mark. It wasn't and she relaxed. A young man sat next to her. He had dark hair, olive skin and a straight nose and so obviously Italian. The man returned her glance and smiled, briefly meeting her eyes, and she looked away quickly.

'E' una bella giornata, sì?'

His voice had a husky tone. He spoke softly and coloured by his Mediterranean accent it was like a caress to Vivien's ears. She looked at him properly before replying. 'Sorry, no Italian.'

'It's a beautiful day, yes?' He translated.

'Yes it's wonderful,' she answered.

'Sei Gia stato qui prima?' he asked and seeing Vivien's confused face, added in English. 'Have you visited the Trevi Fountain before?'

'No, never, but always dreamed I would one day.'

'You must throw a coin into the fountain and make a wish. Then you will come back to Rome one day, and tell the fountain your wish came true.'

Vivien looked at him cynically. 'Really?' she said.

'It's true,' he looked at her expectantly. 'You make your wish now, yes?'

'Oh, alright then,' Vivien laughed. She was grateful for the man's friendliness and took out a small coin from her purse.

'For it to come true you must stand with your back to the fountain and throw the coin over your shoulder.' He said, studying her face.

Receiving attention from an attractive man was something Vivien had long forgotten and she was enjoying it. Her bruises forgotten she took off her hat and stood up obediently with her back to the fountain. 'Here goes,' she said and threw the coin high over her shoulder then turned around quickly to see where it had landed. 'Oh, did I miss?'

'No, it landed right in the middle.' The man assured her.

Vivien sat down again, flattered when the man stayed seated beside her.

'Mi chiamo, Antonio,' he introduced himself and held out his hand.

'Vivien,' she returned taking hold of his hand with a firm grip. 'Pleased to meet you.'

'Sei Cosi Bello,' he said softly, and although Vivien couldn't understand the words, she knew it was a compliment. Was he flirting with her, she wondered. His eyes shone with mischief and she stared back measuring the length of his lashes and the curve of his lips. I'm making a complete fool of myself, she thought smirking, and I don't care.

'You're not on holiday alone, Vivien?' Antonio questioned.

'No, I'm with my husband.' Instinctively Vivien raised her hand to the bruises around her eye and put her hat back on. She glanced at Antonio and wondered if he'd noticed them. She looked to where Mark and Helena had stood earlier but there was no sign of them now.

'He's around here somewhere.' She shifted in her seat to see if she could spot him.

'He shouldn't leave you alone. I'm sad to say there are bad people in Rome, as in any large city. They wouldn't think twice before robbing you of your lovely jewellery.' He spoke earnestly and Vivien was surprised at his concern for her.

Suddenly Antonio began shouting into the crowd. 'Helena, Helena.'

Vivien spotted her husband a few yards away, still in the company of their tour guide, Helena. The name, she supposed, was common enough in Italy but any doubt she had that their Helena could be the object of Antonio's attention disappeared when she saw the girl's reaction to the sound of his voice. She looked up and waved, smiling, and then noticed Vivien and loosened her hold on Mark's arm. Together they walked to where Vivien sat and Antonio stood to meet them. Mark took a quizzical glance at his wife and then sat down beside her, taking Antonio's place.

'Antonio, what are you doing here? Mrs Anderson let me introduce you to my brother.'

Vivien stayed seated and smiled up at them. 'We've already met.'

'Mr Anderson, may I have a word with you?' Antonio gave his sister a quick kiss on the cheek while he waited for a reply.

Mark hesitated and then agreed with a sigh. 'I suppose so.'

'Arrivederci, Vivien.' Antonio called as he walked away with Mark at his heels.

As soon as Antonio and Mark were away from the crowds, Antonio lit a cigarette. He inhaled and let out the smoke. 'You will take the package to this address tomorrow.' He handed Mark a piece of paper. 'The contents will be examined and provided you and Julie have kept your side of the bargain you will be given a key in return.'

'A key, what's that for? I was told I'd be given euros to pay for the painting I was promised.'

'All in good time Mr Anderson. Just make sure you bring the key straight to me.'

'I haven't been able to get hold of Julie, and I still

don't completely trust you, you know. Why should I do as you ask?'

Antonio could feel his patience flagging. The cigarette dangling between his lips began to grow ash. 'I've given you the information you need, what more do you want. The delivery of the package tomorrow is paramount. If you're willing to finish the job you agreed to do, then we'll talk again.'

Mark wasn't happy but he nodded his agreement. Nothing was going to get in the way of his owning a Caravaggio.

CHAPTER 4

On the outskirts of Rome, a grey ribbon road wound its way through the countryside heading towards tall iron gates that guarded the Cortez property thirty kilometres away. An aerial view of the land made the red-tiled roofed house looked like a carbuncle among the lush green landscape of fields and trees. The iron gates, when open, give access to a curving driveway which meant the house couldn't be seen from the road. Six foot high walls surrounded the perimeter, not to keep anyone in but to keep unwanted visitors out. Alonzo Cortez's two bodyguards Matteo and Stephano periodically patrolled the boundary to make sure of it.

Alonzo's wife, Alina, has her own room. She'd given Alonzo, three children. Antonio now aged twenty-eight, Helena twenty-four and, Roberto, a surprise to them all, just twelve. She never objected when her husband laid claim to the master suite for his art studio. Now that Alonzo and Alina were both at an age when sleep seemed more important than sex, she found contentment in the arrangement.

The main objects in Alonzo's studio were a large wooden table, an upright chair, two artist's easels, and furthest away from the window a narrow bed in which he preferred to sleep. Shelves lined one wall. They contained books, and boxes hiding various coloured oil paints. The table was covered in different coloured splashes of paint resembling a larger than life replica of his artists' palette. Jam jars of different sizes held a collection of his brushes. Bristle brushes in a variety of thicknesses and coarseness. Over his usual garb of plaid shirt and blue denim jeans, he wore a sleeved tabard, loose and roomy so that his arms were not restricted in any way.

The vista in Alonzo's studio from the tall wide windows opening on to a narrow stone balcony would be many artists dream, but not for him. His passion for painting was genuine, but bland green landscapes and the clouded sky didn't interest him. He relied on other means to compile his fortune. After his grandfather had passed away, the painting, Boy Peeling Fruit, had been found. Alonzo's father had cleared the house after the funeral and as an afterthought checked the shallow loft above the bedrooms. There he'd come across a piece of sacking and curious he looked inside. His father believed the painting worthless but knew his son, an aspiring artist, would appreciate it. So, when Alonzo came of age he gave it to him as a present.

Alonzo had immediately recognised the subject and eventually, through his contacts in the art world had it authenticated as a genuine early painting by Caravaggio. No one questioned how he had come about it. No one dared question the Cortez family, and the painting, Boy Peeling Fruit, would never be put on display for visitors to see.

On a bright morning, Alonzo opened the studio windows and breathed in the sweet aroma drifting in from climbing jasmine. The stillness of the day was intoxicating and he slipped a cassette into the disc player and stood for a moment listening to the opening cords of his favourite opera, La Traviata. He placed the easels and canvas in various positions in the room to check the amount of light needed for the copy to be perfected and now both easels stood side by side, not quite facing the window. The canvas, already aged and prepared, beckoned him. Smiling, Alonzo picked up his artist's palette. His painting was ready for the final touches. With his finest sable brush, he dabbed small flecks of ivory onto the boy's hairless chest and blended them in little by little. Paint on canvas turned into flesh.

Alonzo had copied the painting, Boy Peeling Fruit so many times he believed his were as good as Caravaggio's early originals. He stood back now and scrutinised the canvas, then smiled and relaxed. It was finished at last. Carefully he unpinned his copy from the easel and carried it over to a low table in front of the open windows to allow it to air and dry. The original painting he left on the spare easel.

Alonzo wiped his brush to remove excess paint and then put it to soak in one of the empty jam jars containing a solvent solution. He took off the smock-like garment and glanced at his watch. It was two o'clock, no wonder he was hungry. He went downstairs to their spotless kitchen and found a plate of sandwiches waiting for him with a pot of fresh coffee. The kitchen still had a slight smell of their previous night's meal. Alina had opened all the windows to let in the fresh air. It wasn't working so Alonzo also opened the patio doors leading to the garden.

Outside he could see Alina and Roberto sitting under a shade reading. Alina had taken to wearing black after her mother passed away three years ago and had never reverted to the fashionable woman he'd married. It didn't matter to Alonzo what his wife wore. She had been a good wife and he loved her. When he glanced out of the window again he was surprised to see his eldest son, Antonio, who waved to him from the garden and began walking towards the house.

'Antonio,' Alonzo said in greeting. 'What brings you here, as if I didn't know?'

'Have you finished it yet?'

'I've just put the final touches to it, and I must say I'm

rather proud of it. Do you want a coffee, are you staying for lunch?' Alonzo said, pouring orange juice into a glass for Roberto.

Antonio nodded. 'The deal is set to go through within the week, earlier than expected.'

His father shrugged non-committal. 'Do you want perfection; well as near as damn it, or do you want an oil painting by numbers? I can produce miracles, but it takes time. Caravaggio was never rushed, and neither will I be.'

'I know, but it can't be helped. Mr Anderson's getting edgy. Please don't be difficult, Papa.'

'As I said, it will be ready in a few days. I will have Matteo take it and have it stored in our usual place until we have been paid. Hopefully, the oil is dry by then.' Alonzo grinned at his son. 'Don't worry, I'm joking. It will be ready on time. Have you arranged for the validation certificate to be signed? Mr Anderson will want that.'

'Yes, it's all in hand.'

'If you feel it important to prove the painting he'll receive is genuine, you can take the original to show him. I'll need it returned immediately, Antonio. I don't feel happy having it out of my sight, but I can trust you, can't I?'

'Absolutely, and thank you,' Antonio replied, relaxing.

CHAPTER 5

The following day at eleven a.m., the tour group was laden with cameras, hats, and bottled water. They piled into the coach like eager school children. Helena checked that the men all wore long trousers and no vest tops and that none of the women had clothing above their knees. Wide scarves and pashminas were handed out to the women who hadn't brought one, as the dress code also specified that women must keep their shoulders and bosom covered in the Vatican.

Vivien watched the pandemonium. Madge, who sat with her husband, Bill in the seat behind her, tapped her shoulder and she turned round to see what she wanted. All Vivian could see in-between the high backed seats was Madge's two eyes reflected behind her spectacles, placed over a small upturned nose and topped with curly grey hair.

'Would you like a scarf,' Madge asked, and without waiting for a reply she handed her one through the gap.

'I already have one, thanks.' Vivien held up hers for Madge to see.

'Oh, that's good. We have to keep our shoulders covered you know.' Madge settled back in her seat satisfied all was well.

They soon arrived at the drop-off point and everyone was given a street map. Helena shouted over the rumble of voices. 'Everyone please listen. Our slot is at two o'clock. I will meet you near the ticket office at one-thirty and you will all be given your tickets for entry into the Vatican then, please keep them safe. You have free time until then. Please be back at Piazza Adriana at five o'clock, where the coach will be waiting to take us back to the hotel. There's going to be quite a crowd today, so I suggest you make your way to St Peter's Basilica immediately, and then you should get a good view of the Pope.'

Helena had already marked their maps where the coach would be standing, so they all set off as if in a parade. Mark held back, waiting to escort Helena.

Vivien linked her arm through David's, and not for the first time wondered what her life would have been like if they had married. 'It says in my guide book that Piazza San Pietro, St Peter's Square, was laid out by Bernini between 1656 and 1667. I can't wait to see it.'

As they neared the piazza David looked up in reverence. 'Oh my, look at that. I'm starting to feel pious again.' In the piazza, space opened out into an enormous ellipse flanked by colonnades. 'It's amazing,' David murmured, exhaling as if he'd been holding his breath.

Vivien laughed, 'but you're not even Catholic.'

'I can still admire architecture though.' David continued to stare, looking up at the grandeur of it all.

Couples from their party passed them a few yards away and waved. Madge shouted over. 'Isn't it marvellous?'

David took photos of the Swiss Guards in their flounced uniforms of cobalt blue and yellow, and Vivien posed for him with the sweep of apostles atop the colonnades behind her. Suddenly the crowds began to thicken and David took hold of Vivien's arm.

'Let's see if we can get nearer to the front, we'll have a better view.' Trying to keep together they edged their way through the crowds.

Despite their efforts, they only managed to get as far as the middle of the gathering, and behind them, the mass of people continued to push closer. At noon a great cheer rose up and high up on a small balcony stood the Pope dressed in his celestial robes. From where they stood he looked like a doll's house figure, but when his voice began to boom out over loudspeakers and the sudden silence of the crowd, the tiny figure became colossal.

After the blessing, David suggested lunch in a nearby restaurant. Mark was nowhere to be seen and with so many people milling about Vivien knew it would be almost impossible to find him, so she agreed. It was nearing two o'clock by the time they finished their meal and they quickly made their way to the ticket office.

Helena, with Mark by her side, handed them their tickets.

'You cut that fine,' Mark said snappily.

The rest of their group were waiting in anticipation and at two o'clock in groups of two or three, they entered the Vatican.

Inside St. Peter's church, eleven chapels and forty-five alters contained abundant precious works of art. Two passageways converged under Michelangelo's huge dome. Vivien didn't know where to look first and wandered about enthralled. With David by her side, she entered the Sistine Chapel, and neither spoke. The silence was tangible. They stood on an intricately tiled floor in blues, ochre and different shades of grey. It seemed sacrilege to walk on it and Vivien felt the urge to levitate. They were surrounded by a haze of blue. Michelangelo di Lodovico had painted wonderful Renaissance scenes in-between intricate stone arches, borders and ledges. The scenes depicted worshipers, men and women, wearing clothes in colours complementing the colours on the tiled floor. At the far end of the room, through a trellis screen, marble steps led up to the scene of Christ on the cross. To the sides and rear of Christ, ogres lived in caves and fought in boats. Vivien could hear small gasps coming from David beside her.

'Are you alright,' she whispered. He turned his face towards her and she saw his eyes misty with tears. Vivien gave his arm a quick squeeze. 'Come on let's finish the rest of our tour.' She told him quietly.

Vivien left David to his own devices and followed the directions to the Doria Pamphilj Gallery, which was top of her list to explore. Here was where Caravaggio's masterpieces were on display, and she was sure this was where Mark would be.

Vivien came to a centre point, a T junction with corridors branching off to left and right. She turned right and walked along the corridor acutely aware of the sound of her footsteps in the silence and seclusion. A third of the way along she heard voices, murmurings, which halted her.

Was it chanting? Had she accidentally happened upon priests in prayer? Vivien couldn't determine from which direction the murmuring came. Nearby two sarcophagi flanked the entrance to an Egyptian display and through the opening, she saw a tall obelisk taking centre stage. Besides the obelisk stood two men, she didn't recognise the taller of the two, but the shorter man was Mark.

Since arriving in Rome Mark had been acting weird, furtive and preoccupied. Vivien wondered if the man he was with had something to do with it. Curious, she knelt behind the nearest Sarcophagus and listened to their conversation hoping no one came along to see her crouched there.

It seemed silly, even to Vivien that she felt the need to hide from her husband.

'There must be some misunderstanding.' Mark was saying impatiently.

'You are Mark Anderson?' the question was asked in perfect English, cultured, masculine, but cold.

'Yes.'

'My name is Jack Tyler. Julie Merriton asked you to bring a package through customs I believe.'

'Look, I don't care who you are, or what you believe. If you don't mind I'd like to continue to enjoy my tour of the Vatican.' Mark was completely bewildered. He had telephoned Julie several times that morning. Eventually, he resorted to leaving messages on the answering machine but as yet she hadn't got back to him.

'Do you know what is in the package?'

'I don't know what you're talking about.' Mark blustered.

'Has anyone made contact with you, a stranger perhaps?'

Mark began to walk in Vivien's direction, a few more steps and he'd see her. Vivien held her breath, not daring to move.

'I wouldn't advise playing games with me, Mr Anderson.'

'Are you threatening me?' Mark demanded.

'No, Mr Anderson. Perhaps this will explain my interest.'

Vivien peeped over the top of the stone sarcophagus wondering in which direction it was best to flee. She watched the tall man pass a card to Mark and even though she couldn't see her husband's expression as he read the words, she sensed his uneasiness. To Vivien's relief the man walked away in the opposite direction and exited the Egyptian museum through a door she couldn't see. After a few minutes, she heard his footsteps in the passageway behind her. Vivien knew she had to make a move quickly before Mark discovered her so bending low she backed away. Keeping her distance from the man walking ahead, she followed, glancing over her shoulder occasionally anxious in case Mark had seen or heard her.

Vivien turned a corner and was dismayed to find David in animated conversation with the same man who'd spoken to Mark a few minutes earlier. Both stood admiring, Raphael's *Transfiguration*.

'There you are,' David said as soon as he saw her. He placed an arm around Vivien's shoulders when she reached his side.

'I got a bit lost.' Vivien glanced at the other man. She didn't recognise him from their hotel nor remembered seeing him on the coach. Clutching David's arm she asked. 'Have you seen enough?'

David took the hint. 'It's time to head back to the coach now anyway.' David told her. He nodded goodbye to the man standing by his side and Vivien had the impression it wasn't the first time he and David had met. A look passed between them, as though an understanding or agreement had been made. Something in the man's expression unnerved her.

Mark exited the Vatican and began the walk back to Piazza Adriana where the coach would be parked. He replayed the conversation he'd just had with the stranger over and over in his mind. He'd nearly had a coronary when he'd read the words printed on the man's business card. Julie had reassured him everything was in order, so why was a customs and excise investigator breathing down his neck. He desperately needed to speak to Julie to confirm Antonio was legit. If he was to deliver the diamonds to the address Antonio had given him, he was running out of time.

Besides his frustration, Mark was uneasy. He had no guarantee that the painting, Boy Peeling Fruit, was by Caravaggio, or that it even existed. Why wasn't Julie returning his calls? Had she set him up?

Mark looked over his shoulder. There was no sign of

anyone following him but that didn't mean anything. Unnerved, Mark slipped into a side street, taking a short cut instead of staying on the main road. After a few yards, he turned again to check if anyone was following him and saw a tall man wearing a dark suit turn the corner and hurry towards him. Mark began to run. Soon he was on a busy thoroughfare and in a state of agitation. Without looking where he was going he began to cross a road. Too late, he heard, and then saw the motorbike and rider speeding towards him. The collision knocked Mark into the air and he landed with a thud in the gutter at the side of the road. His head pressed against a grid he listened to the rush of water gurgling in the drains below. Like music with no rhythm, symbols crashing. He felt his head filling, felt himself falling, becoming part of the rushing torrent. Hands reached down and tried to pull him up and he screamed out in pain before he felt himself sink into the turbulent flow.

Mark woke up in the hospital and saw Vivien sitting next to the bed, her face in repose. She looked at peace and guilt reared its ugly head again. What had he gotten them into? There was a time when he'd prayed she would up and leave him, find herself someone else to fuss over. But no, ever the loyal wife was Vivien. Although if Mark was honest with himself, he knew it was her love for their daughter, Isobel, that had kept them together, rather than any sentiment for him. He attempted to sit but the heavy plaster cast around his leg was cumbersome.

Vivien opened her eyes. 'You're awake,' she said unnecessarily. 'How are you?'

'I'm bloody marvellous, thanks. I've got a broken leg, two cracked ribs and a gash on my arm that needed stitches. How do you think I feel?' Mark snapped back and instantly regretted it. Why did he do it he wondered as he watched Vivien's face fall?

'Sorry.' Vivien fumbled in her bag for something to do, and to compose herself.

'No, I'm sorry.' An apology from Mark was something Vivien hadn't expected and she looked at him in surprise. 'Forgive me. I shouldn't take my anger out on you.'

'What happened? I was told you were involved in a road accident and were asking for me. Helena brought me straight here. She's worried about you too.'

'Is she still here, I need to talk to her.' Mark looked at the door as if expecting Helena to walk in.

'No, she dropped me off at the hospital on her way home.'

'Blast it, but never mind that. I'm glad you're here. Look, Vivien, I need you to do something for me. It's very important and I can't go myself, not in this state. I wouldn't normally dream of asking or putting you in possible da.......' Mark stopped himself in time.

'Putting me in what, danger, is that what you were going to say?' Vivien questioned.

'No, no, putting you to the trouble, that's all.' Mark felt himself blush. Not because it was necessary to lie to Vivien, but because she was right. She could find herself in danger. The motorbike hadn't tried to slow down and hadn't stopped. Mark was convinced that his so-called accident was intentional. Someone was trying to stop him from delivering the package, a warning perhaps, but from whom? Mark gave Vivien a wry smile. 'I've got myself into a bit of bother. An old friend asked me to bring a package to Rome and deliver it to an address in Ponte Casilino. It's quite important. Will you take it for me?'

'Please don't tell me you smuggled drugs through security at the airport, Mark?'

Mark wanted to say, I didn't Vivien, but you might have. He hadn't considered the package might contain drugs and not diamonds as Julie had told him. Again, the question of trusting Julie bothered him. He pushed the likelihood of her being mixed up in drug dealing out of his mind for now, and smiled at Vivien, desperately needing her on his side. 'It's nothing like that. Do you remember me telling you about Julie Merriton, she deals in art and antiques? She gave me my first job and a step up the ladder in the antique business. It was through her I came to appreciate oil paintings and Old Masters.'

'Yes, I remember. Didn't she dump you after a rather sordid affair?'

'I wouldn't put it quite like that, but yes, all right, we had an affair. She used me if you want to know the truth, but it was well over before we met and I hadn't heard from her until a few weeks before we came on holiday.'

'I see. So our holiday was all about doing an ex-lover a favour, and smuggling of all things. What did she offer you in return, the opportunity to rekindle the old flame? I know you, Mark; you wouldn't have agreed if there wasn't something in it for you.'

Mark was surprised. His wife hadn't spoken to him like that in years. Perhaps she felt brave enough because he was incapacitated. She sounded like the no-nonsense woman he'd fallen for. Her beauty and intellect had enticed him, but her resilient spirit had clinched his love for her. These days he would normally have backhanded her for speaking to him like that. Mark tried to grasp her hand but couldn't quite reach it. 'I had already booked our holiday months before Julie contacted me, Vivien. Close the blinds and I'll explain,' he said. After Vivien had done what was asked she sat down beside the bed again. 'You'll never believe it when I tell you. I've got the chance to purchase a Caravaggio, one of his early pieces.

Just think of it Vivien, us owning a Caravaggio painting.'

'How on earth can you afford it?'

Mark waved her concerns away determined not to let her put the dampeners on his good fortune. 'It's all taken care of. All I have to do is deliver the payment, which is why I must get the package to the address in Ponte Casilino.' Mark didn't bother to mention he had re-mortgaged Lilac House or the money he'd loaned from David and given him twenty-five per cent of the business as surety.

Mark waved at his broken leg. 'Because of this, I need you to take it for me.'

'How big is the package, is it heavy?' Vivien asked.

'It's small enough to fit in your handbag. At the moment it's hidden inside one of my brown leather brogues.' Mark re-assured her.

'If it isn't drugs, what does the package contain?'

'Diamonds actually, and it's all above board. I have certificates to prove it.'

'All right,' Vivien reluctantly agreed, and then had a thought. 'Is it okay if David comes with me?'

'No, definitely not,' Mark shouted.

A nurse opened the door and looked in. 'Is everything alright Mr Anderson? Do you need more painkillers?' she asked.

'I'm fine, thank you, nurse,' Mark replied, and waited until she had left the room and closed the door again. 'No one must know about this, Vivien. I'm not supposed to tell you, but now with this, I have no choice.' Mark indicated his plastered leg again. He leaned back against the pillows before giving the rest of his instructions. 'Now, after you've been back to the hotel to get the package, take it to an address in Ponte Casilino. Look in my cream linen jacket, the address is in the breast pocket. Go by bus. I've looked up the times and it only takes about twenty-five minutes. The address is a short walk, about ten minutes away from the bus stop. Get the bus back too. If you're offered a lift or a taxi, refuse it you hear?'

Vivien thought it mean of Mark not to offer to pay for a taxi but she nodded in agreement. 'I'll go tomorrow morning after breakfast.'

Mark was silent for a while. 'It has got to be delivered today, Vivien. Otherwise, we could be in more trouble. Promise me you will go today. In fact, go now.'

CHAPTER 6

Vivien

Back at the hotel, I retrieved the package from Mark's shoe. I kept asking myself what sort of person dealt in smuggled goods. The answer was obvious, a criminal, and I was on my way to meet one. Scenarios played out in my mind. I was murdered and my body dumped in a skip. This possibility had me wondering what Mark and Isobel would wear to my funeral and if they'd remember what flowers I liked. I might survive and drag my raped and broken body out of the skip. How Mark would hate me for failing and losing him the Caravaggio.

This is what happens when you read too many crime novels.

Failing wasn't an option so I needed to plan. The scrap of paper I'd found in Mark's jacket with its scattering of lines, o's and x's was so obscure that it could have been a game of noughts and crosses, except for a few letters, C and PC. I decided first to plan my route. I'd come up with the password for Mark's Apple iPad when he'd originally bought it, and thankfully he hadn't bothered to change it. I typed in the password, Merisi67, Caravaggio's surname and the last two digits of Marks year of birth and *Voilà*. Google maps soon found me Ponte Casilino and according to the directions it was pretty straightforward as Mark had said. I made a few notes of the bus numbers I'd need to look out for and began to feel somewhat relieved. 'You can do this Vivien,' I told myself.

The bus dropped me off in Ponte Casilino to the sound of a train. I couldn't see it but a railway track was close by and the volume of clattering went on forever. Up to now, everything had gone as planned but as I looked around at the number of roads and streets darting off in all directions my heart sank. Around me tall six storied apartment buildings towered over me, shops on the ground floor. The smell of petrol and diesel fumes filled my nose and throat as motorbikes, scooters and cars chugged while waiting at traffic lights on red. The main road was wide, and in the middle two circles of traffic, cones were being used as a small makeshift roundabout. A wide pedestrian crossing stopped short from the pavement on the other side of the road by at least two metres. I thought about crossing the road to a pharmacy to ask for directions but the traffic began to move and the sound of car horns honking in my ears put me off. I took the scrap of paper out of my trouser pocket and once again tried to make sense of it.

I figured out PC represented Ponte Casilino, that much was obvious, but the surrounding roads didn't correspond with my map. I studied it more closely. If one of the O's was a B it could represent the bus stop, and the arrow pointing to the right was the direction in which I should go. I decided to give my intuition a try and set off.

I reached the end of the block and turned a corner. Multi-coloured graffiti painted on a long concrete wall hit me. Some of the artwork looked obscene. It included large Italian words I couldn't interpret but it didn't take much imagination to know what they meant. I hurried past. The long road stretched before me, so much for Mark's assurance, it was only a short walk from the bus stop. Perhaps this wasn't the right way after all.

Before I left the hotel I'd attempted to dress in what I thought a middle-aged Italian woman might wear. My disguise was black linen trousers and a white tee shirt.

The probable giveaway was my bright pink cardigan and gold coloured sandals but it was the best I could come up with at such short notice. I silently prayed I wouldn't draw too much attention.

I looked around me at square grey and brown three-story flat-roofed buildings that lined the road. Faded and peeling wooden shutters outlined the windows. A Vespa scooter zipped past me, its noise a screech in my ears invading my thoughts. Halfway down the road, the pavements petered out, as did the street lights. Clouds were gathering, the sun had dipped lower.

The directional arrows on the scrap of paper took me into a small courtyard that was nothing more than a quadrangle behind another block of apartments. Here, some had balconies and makeshift washing lines. I saw a painted chair on one and on another, the clothesline had coloured pegs holding vests. I could smell herbs and lamb stew. What stood out most was the array of sky dishes, miniature moons dotted here and there. A latticework of wrought iron secured the windows on the first floor. On-street level a row of garages with some doors looking as though they had never been opened. A set of stone steps led me to the address I needed and when I reached the top I walked to the end of an open balcony. A door inset and partly hidden in shadow had a hand-painted capital C on it. I had arrived. I knocked twice and waited. There was no light in the window but after a few minutes, I heard a noise and the sound of a bolt being drawn. The door opened an inch and my stomach churned as the smell of garlic, fried food and body odour seeped through the crack.

'Hello, I'm Vivien Anderson, scusa, non parlo Italiano.'

'Anderson, Oi vey, I expected a man, eh?' The door opened wider and a slightly stooped man ushered me into a small square vestibule. He pushed past me to open another door and switch on a lamp. From the low light, I was able to see the man properly for the first time and while I took in his stout frame and bearded face I saw that he was dressed in black. He wore a blue kippah on his head and matted ringlets fell to just below his ears on either side of his face. He studied me in the same way and smiled showing gold incisors on each side of his stained teeth. His smile never reached his hooded eyes and in the gloom, I thought he looked a little sinister which didn't help settle my nerves or my thumping heartbeat. Once again I wondered what on earth Mark had been thinking. There again, Mark was in the hospital safe and sound. I was the one in possible danger.

'How did you get here, eh?'

I found that I liked the man's Jewish accent and as he was attempting to be friendly, I smiled at him. 'By bus to Via le Spezia, then I walked the rest of way here. You know why I'm here don't you, Mister....'

'No Mister, just Caplan. Where is your husband? He should have come yesterday, not you today. What's going on, eh?' The Jewish man lifted a poker from the grate and began moving the charred remains of a burnt log to make room for another. The warmth and light from the fire disappeared, replaced by grey smoke which made the room gloomier.

'My husband has had an accident. He's in hospital, so he asked me to bring this to you in his place.' I took the package from my bag and handed it to Caplan.

'Here sit, sit. You want a drink, my dear, eh?' Caplan began clearing books off a worn and stained sofa to make a place for me to sit down. He reached for a bottle and two glasses from a sideboard and poured us both a drink. The glass was grubby but not wanting to offend him I took a mouthful and then almost choked. It was a neat whisky. Caplan laughed and swallowed his in one gulp, then poured another.

While I sat with the glass in my hand, Caplan perched on a chair next to a small side table near the fire. Neither of us spoke. Aware of the time and my journey home, I broke the silence. 'Mr Caplan, my husband told me I'm to collect something from you in return.'

'Caplan, just Caplan you hear, are you deaf?' Caplan shouted then put down his glass with a loud sigh. 'What sort of accident?' I must have looked blank or perhaps he thought I was deaf because he raised his voice yet again. 'Your husband, what happened to him?'

'Oh! It was a road accident. A motorbike ran into him. He was lucky, only a broken leg and a few broken ribs.'

'Are you sure it was an accident? Perhaps next time he won't be so lucky, eh?'

'What do you mean?' It sounded like a threat but I didn't challenge him further. Caplan ignored my question and began opening the package. He lifted out a drawstring bag and looked inside, then tipped a few of the contents into the palm of his hand. At best I'd expected to see a piece of jewellery, gold embedded with precious gems, at worst, small plastic packages containing white powder, but what Caplan held looked like dull opaque stones.

'I check these, you wait here,' he said, slipping the stones back into the bag and going into an adjoining room.

A dull strip of light outlined the door and I focused on that while I sipped my whisky and waited. The tick of a large brown Bakelite clock drew my attention. It stood amid numerous porcelain vases and a bronze sculpture arranged alongside the whisky bottle on a sideboard. I looked at my watch to check the time, eight forty-five, and the old clock agreed. Ten minutes later Caplan emerged from the other room, the drawstring bag in one hand an envelope in the other.

'They are beautiful, perfect, and exquisite. I am satisfied.' His brusque tone of voice had changed, replaced by a conciliatory manner, friendlier. He held out his hand for me to shake and then gave me an envelope.

'Can I ask what kind of stones they are?'

'Diamonds, my dear, diamonds. They're uncut but flawless, see.' Caplan took out one of the stones and passed it to me to examine. 'To the naked eye, it looks dull and ordinary, eh.' Before I could answer he'd whipped it out of my hand and put it back into the bag.

'What is in the envelope?' I asked him. It didn't seem much in return for a bag of perfect diamonds.

Caplan looked at me for a moment, his head on one side as if considering something, and then he said 'I've given you a key, a number and an address. Keep them both safe. You leave now. I'll telephone for a taxi.'

'Thank you anyway but I'll get the bus,' I assured him quickly, thinking how preferable a taxi would be.

'No, no, it isn't safe, my dear. Bad men, thieves, I must insist.'

I agreed and thanked him, and then asked. 'Use la toilette.' Caplan showed me the way and I took the envelope and my handbag with me.

I was glad to be out of Caplan's apartment and away from the man. I waited near the entrance to the courtyard for the taxi, but after five minutes and still no sign of it, I decided to walk. It wasn't long before I could see cars and buses intermittently passing the end of the long road and it spurred me on.

It was cooler now and dark clouds hung low threatening rain. I hadn't quite reached the pavement where street lights were, and due to be lit, when somewhere behind me a car door slammed. Heavy footsteps quickened their pace as they got nearer, and I edged sideways towards a wall to give room for them to pass. Passing me wasn't their intention. The attack came quickly and caught me off guard. I felt a sharp blow to the side of my head as I was slammed into the side of the wall and then pushed with such force my knees gave way and I toppled forward. Arms outstretched I tried to protect my face and I cried out in pain when my assailant wrenched my handbag from my grasp. I lay facing the road and listened as the heavy footsteps receded. I felt too shocked to move and sobbed into the dirt.

Before I had time to recover, a second car drew to a halt a metre away. From where I lay sprawled I could see the wheels. I tried to lift myself up, and then I heard shouting and the screech of tyres. I lay back down again too terrified to move.

A cool hand touched my forehead and I felt breath on my face. Woody aftershave reminded me of nutmegs and my father who always kept one in his pocket.

'Mrs Anderson, let me help you up.'

CHAPTER 7

The nurse at Mark's side offered him a wheelchair which he refused. Instead, he stood cautiously, a crutch resting under each armpit. He took a tentative step with his good right leg and as though with a mind of its own his left leg followed and he breathed out in relief. He managed to get into the elevator without a mishap and out again on the ground floor of the hospital. A taxi, pre-ordered, was waiting for him. He gave the driver the name of the hotel and sat back awkwardly. His left leg in bright blue plaster from above the knee to his ankle stuck out unbending like an alien growth.

The hotel lobby was unusually quiet and empty of tourists. Mark spoke to the man at reception and asked to speak to Helena and he was disappointed to hear she was out on a tour, although not surprised. He eyed the elevator on the far side of the lobby and half-heartedly struggled his way towards it.

Mark thought it unusually dark for the time of day when he opened the door to their hotel room and so switched on the light, then stood open-mouthed in the doorway. The mattress tipped up off the bed, now stood up against the window blocking out the natural daylight. The wardrobe doors were open and a chaos of clothes and shoes were strewn across the floor. The drawers in the bedside tables and a chest of drawers had been pulled out and lay scattered, the contents tipped unceremoniously to join the rest of their possessions on the floor.

Mark picked up a table lamp and placed it back on one of the bedside tables. He lowered himself down onto the hard bed frame letting his crutches fall on top of all the debris. He sat at a loss looking around the room and noticed their suitcases ripped apart. After a few minutes he roused himself, the shock and panic he'd felt moments before was replaced by rage. He picked up the telephone receiver and pressed the number for the reception. It was answered after a few rings.

'Reception, how can I help you?'

'It's Mark Anderson. You had better send security up to our room straight away.'

'Is there a problem?'

'Yes, there bloody well is a problem, so be quick about it.' Mark slammed down the phone. He held his head in his hands, near to tears. He began to think about possible explanations and could only come up with one, an explanation that turned Mark's blood cold. He sat immobile until the Security Manager appeared outside the open door.

'Whatever happened here?'

'You tell me,' Mark said picking up his crutches and struggling to stand.

'Mr Anderson, where are you going? We need to get this sorted out.'

'Do what you have to do and get us another room. I'll be in the bar.' Mark step dragged his way across the room and into the corridor, leaving the bewildered man in the middle of all the clutter.

It was too early for alcohol to be served in the hotel, but the barman, not yet on duty, obliged Mark who downed a second straight whisky with more painkillers than allowed. Only then did he feel ready to speak to Antonio.

'Buon Giorno,' Antonio answered after the first ring.

'Mark Anderson here, I need to see you.'

'You sent your wife to deliver the diamonds. That wasn't part of our arrangement.'

'I know, wait don't hang up.' Mark shouted. 'I was involved in an accident yesterday and ended up in the hospital. I've got a broken leg and cracked ribs. I'm on crutches, so I had to ask Vivien to take the package in my place. Hello, are you still there?'

'I am listening.'

'The hospital insisted I stay in overnight. I was discharged this morning and I arrived back at the hotel about an hour ago to find our room had been ransacked. Antonio, there is no sign of Vivien.' Mark could hear noises in the background and he wondered who else was there.

'What do you expect me to do about it?'

'Nothing, I'm just explaining my predicament. There's something else. Just before I had my accident a man came up to me in the Vatican and began asking me questions about the diamonds I brought through customs. It unnerved me I can tell you. I need to see you, Antonio. I want to know what is going on.'

'Did the man give you his name?' Antonio was taking more notice and he sounded worried.

From the altered tone of Antonio's voice, Mark relaxed a little. He sensed Antonio's full attention at last. 'Yes, his name is Jack Tyler,' Mark replied. 'Have you heard of him?'

'I'll pick you up outside your hotel in an hour, and Mr Anderson, I suggest you try to locate your wife.'

The building where Antonio lived was surrounded by others like it. Tall multi-windowed apartment blocks with shutters to most windows and wrought-iron balconies. Mark struggled up the few steps to the communal front door while Antonio punched in a key code and then held it open and waited for Mark to enter. Once inside, Antonio began walking up a curved staircase.

'Is there an elevator, I'll never manage the stairs on my crutches?'

Antonio stopped, his hand resting on a wooden bannister. He pointed to metal doors set into the wall behind Mark and then jogged on up. 'The second floor,' he called down, as an afterthought.

Mark had never felt so vulnerable and didn't like the way Antonio looked down on him, and not just from the height of the staircase.

Inside Antonio's luxurious apartment paintings filled two of the walls. Mark recognized a Monet, Degas, Paul Cezanne and, hardly believing his eyes, a Vermeer. Facing him two large ceiling to floor glazed doors opened onto a balcony and soft voile curtains swayed gently in a light breeze. A wide arch led into a bright modern kitchen where Antonio had begun to make coffee.

Mark perched on the arm of a leather sofa. He didn't trust he'd be able to get up again if he let himself sink into the soft seats. Antonio handed Mark his coffee and sat facing him on the sofa's twin opposite.

'Am I right in thinking these are all reproductions?' Mark asked pointing to Antonio's display of artwork.

Antonio looked at his paintings. 'You're the expert. Do you consider them fakes?'

'Well they're good, I'll give you that.'

'If you look at them closely you may be astonished to find that you can't tell the difference. If you're the connoisseur of fine art you claim to be, I challenge you to pick out a fake among them.'

Mark heaved himself up again and began examining the paintings. After a few minutes in front of each one, he shook his head. 'As I thought, all fake.'

'If my paintings were on display in a museum would you still believe that? Or is it because they are in the home of an ordinary Italian I wonder.'

Mark couldn't help being impressed by the clarity of colour and detail in the paintings, or the lavishness of his surroundings. He shook his head. 'No, I don't think I would.'

'So, Mr Anderson, how much would you give to own a genuine Caravaggio?'

Mark took a sip of his coffee. He swallowed too quickly almost choking. In between a coughing fit, he managed to splutter. 'Is that meant to be a joke? I've paid for a genuine Caravaggio, and by God, I'd better get one.'

'Would you like to see it?' Antonio asked enjoying the game of cat and mouse he was playing with the pompous man.

'Do you have it here?' Mark felt his palms begin to sweat.

'Yes.' Antonio walked over to a corner of the room where a large sideboard was draped with a white cotton sheet. He lifted the sheet away and uncovered the painting which lay underneath. 'What's your impression of this?'

Mark went over to where Antonio stood and bent over to see the painting. Suddenly he was lightheaded and his good leg began to shake. He wasn't sure if it was the effect the painting had on him or the pain killers mixed with whisky he'd taken earlier.

Antonio put a hand on Mark's arm to steady him. 'Are you all right?' he asked, somewhat amused by the effect the painting had on him.

Mark looked at him and managed a nod, his eyes moist. 'Boy Peeling Fruit,' he said.

'Yes, this is the Caravaggio you were promised. You can't have it just yet, I'm showing it to you to alleviate any doubts you may have.'

Mark couldn't take his eyes away from the painting that would soon belong to him. 'I'm satisfied, thank you.'

Antonio gave Mark a few more minutes to admire the masterpiece then changed the subject. 'About Jack Tyler, he's a customs and excise investigator, although you already know that, don't you. It's why you insisted Vivien take the diamonds to the jeweller, Caplan. It had nothing to do with your broken leg. A taxi would have taken you door to door. After I spoke to you on the telephone earlier, I made a few inquiries. Vivien delivered the package successfully and in return was given a locker key with a receipt and the information needed to obtain the payment for the painting.

'Thank goodness.' Mark said, relieved.

'I've also learned that she was mugged on her way home. Her handbag was stolen in the process. I can only assume that the reason your hotel room was ransacked was that the thieves didn't get what they wanted from your wife. So the questions we must ask ourselves are. Where is Vivien, and is the key still in her possession?'

Mark paled. 'Vivien was mugged? Good heavens, is she all right? Have the police been notified?'

'Are you a fool? Of course the police haven't been notified.'

'All right, but what about Vivien, do you know where she is?'

'Probably back at the hotel by now, and if she is, Helena will look after her.

'Have you any idea who might have attacked her?'

'Did anyone else know she was delivering the diamonds last night?'

'I warned her not to tell anyone.'

Antonio had liked Vivien and wished her no harm. It was regrettable that Mark had involved her. 'As far as we know the mugging may have been done by opportunists, and the ransacking of your hotel room a coincidence. Now, do you want this painting or not. You decide.'

Mark accepted that Antonio was most probably right, and Vivien would be safely back at the hotel by now. 'What do I have to do?'

'When you see, Vivien, get the key and bring it to me, along with the rest of the information Caplan gave her. In exchange, you will get a key to another locker that will contain the painting. By the way, did Tyler give you his card?'

A frown creased Mark's forehead. 'Yes, he did, why?'

'It will have his telephone number on it. Contact Mr Tyler and arrange to meet him, your choice where.'

'What for, what do I say to him?'

'He'll believe you've decided to give him the information he wants, so you don't need to worry about that. Just let me know the time and place and I will take care of the rest. You have twenty-four hours, Mr Anderson. If the key isn't in my possession by then and Tyler is still making a nuisance of himself, then the deal is off. Just so you know the people I work for don't take kindly to being double-crossed and you'll be watching your back for the rest of your life if you do.' Antonio telephoned for a taxi to take Mark back to Hotel Muscatello.

Antonio's next call was to his father. 'I'm on my way home.'

Alonzo stood outside the house on the wide marble steps eagerly waiting for his son's arrival. As soon as the Fiat Panda came into view, he hurried down ready to open the car door and only when he held the painting in his hands again did he feel relaxed.

'How did it go?' Alonzo asked, but didn't wait for his son to reply. Instead, he hurried upstairs to his studio. He took down the fake Boy Peeling Fruit painting from the easel and carefully rolled it up before placing it on the table. It had properly dried now and soon would be put into a container ready to be transported to the rail terminal storage locker. Happily, he put the original Caravaggio in its rightful place on the easel. Alonzo sighed. Everything was back to how it should be.

Antonio had forgotten it was his father's birthday that day, and it was only when Helena arrived a few hours later, burdened with presents, that he remembered. He felt guilty that he hadn't even bought a card and grabbed Helena as she came into the house. 'Will you add my name onto his card,' he asked.

After dinner, they moved from the dining room into the outside patio area where Alina had put up coloured lights and balloons. Presents were handed to Alonzo, who opened them and thanked his family for their thoughtfulness. Antonio stood up amid the happy chatter.

'Happy birthday Father, and forgive me. I ordered you a present online but it hasn't arrived in time, I'm sorry.' Alonzo smiled at his eldest son knowing full well that he'd forgotten and he raised his glass in a mock salute.

Antonio and Helena stayed the night in the rooms they'd had since childhood, and little had changed. Rosy wallpaper still clung to the walls of Helena's room and Antonio's posters of sports cars hung above his bed in pride of place.

At breakfast the following morning Alina looked worried. 'Your father is unwell,' she told her children. 'He doesn't want to, but I think we should take him to the hospital to be checked.'

'What's wrong with him?' Helena asked, just beating

Antonio to it.

'Chest pain and he seems to think it is just indigestion after last night's heavy meal. I'm not so sure, though. Will you take us, Helena, please?'

'Of course, I'll get my bag.' Helena rushed off to her bedroom to pick up her stuff.

Outside, Antonio helped his father into the car's front passenger seat. Alina and Roberto sat in the back. 'I'll call you,' Helena said to reassure Antonio, before driving away.

All Antonio could think about at that moment was the arrangement he and his father had made with Mark Anderson. He wasn't about to allow Alonzo's somewhat dubious illness to get in the way of it and he knew it was up to him to see the deal through. In any case, his father wouldn't thank him if he ended up two hundred thousand pounds poorer

Antonio climbed the stairs to Alonzo's studio and studied the genuine Caravaggio painting still on the easel. Believing it to be the one his father had just completed, he stood admiring it, appreciating what he thought was his father's work. Antonio took the painting down from the easel and rolled it up. In a corner, numerous cardboard cylindrical containers were stacked ready for use. He picked out one which was the right size and slipped the rolled canvas into it, securing the opening at the top with a lid.

Antonio drove to the Rail Terminal at Piazza Dei Cinquecento in Rome in high spirits. The painting would soon be safely at the rail terminal's Baggage Storage ready for collection.

CHAPTER 8

Vivien

I must have passed out because I awoke to find myself sitting in the passenger seat of a stationary car. I felt dizzy and sick and tried to open the door but it was locked, so I leaned over and spewed up in the foot-well. The pain in my head was piercing and I fought to remember how I had got here. The man in the driver's seat handed me a wad of tissues and I took them gratefully. He got out of the car and came round to the passenger side and opened the door. He helped me out and I stood on shaking legs and watched as he took out the ruined car mat and wiped the seat clean.

'Are you okay now?' He asked.

I'd watched films where people were kidnapped and I knew I mustn't look at him. If I did he would have to kill me, so I turned away and nodded. The car's headlights lit up the landscape in front of us. Dark blocks of distant houses shone the odd light from a window, and above, a three-quarter pale moon hung low over fields that rolled away in all directions. The car was parked on a dirt track and I couldn't see any lights illuminating a main road or motorway. The only sound, other than insects clicking and nattering in the fields, was my laboured breathing. I cleaned myself up as best I could but I couldn't stop shaking. I'd faced Mark in his fury and knew the consequences of it, but I'd never been as frightened as I was now.

My face still averted, I asked. 'Where are we?'

'On the outskirts of Rome,' the man stated as if I should have realised.

I felt his eyes on me, studying, contemplating, and although it wasn't a cold evening I shivered. I was alone in the middle of nowhere with a stranger.

'Get back in the car now,' he demanded. There was nowhere else to go so I did as he commanded.

'Why won't you look at me?' He asked sounding amused.

'If I do you'll have to kill me, right?' I continued to look away but the view outside wasn't encouraging and my eyes refused to shut.

'Not necessarily.'

'Well if you're thinking of having sex with me, I wouldn't bother. I'm not very good at it apparently.'

'Is that so?'

'It is.'

'For what it's worth, I don't want to have sex with you. All I want is to ask you a few questions.'

I couldn't resist not looking at him any longer and I stole a glance. Although it was dark in the car there was something familiar about him.

'You're not a policeman, are you? I don't have to tell you anything.'

The man exhaled a sigh. 'Why did you visit Mr Caplan?'

'Who's that?'

The man began muttering under his breath, and I could tell I was testing his patience. 'A few days ago you carried a bag of uncut diamonds through customs at Manchester airport, and this evening you took them to a jeweller. He gave you something in return, what was it. You were attacked for it, don't you remember? I found you lying in the gutter and brought you here.'

Now I remembered. It accounted for the headache and the enormous lump on the side of my head. 'How do

I know it wasn't you who attacked me?'

'I can assure you it wasn't. Did you have anything of value in your handbag, other than the item the jeweller, Mr Caplan gave you?'

'No, just my hotel key card, some Euros for the bus fare, tissues, oh, and my mobile phone.' The thought of my precious iPhone in the hands of a thug made me feel nauseous again.

'So Mr Caplan did give you something? What was it?'

'If you wanted to help me why didn't you take me straight to the hospital, or back to my hotel? You seem to know a good deal about me so you probably know where I'm staying.'

'I do. Now tell me, what did Mr Caplan give you? I'm not going to harm you.'

'All right, yes, he gave me an envelope. Are you satisfied? Anyway, it's just Caplan. He doesn't like to be called Mr.'

'Mrs Anderson, you're playing a very precarious game.' The man put his hand into his jacket pocket and for a moment I thought he was going to pull out a gun. Instead, he handed me his wallet and a passport. 'Open the passport,' he said, and I did.

'Look at the photo, is that me?'

'Yes,' I answered, with a sinking sensation in my stomach.

'Read out loud what it says on the business card in my wallet. My driving licence is there too which also has my name and a photograph of me.'

I cleared my throat while I skimmed the words and took in what they meant. 'It states, Jack Tyler, HMS Customs and Excise Investigator.' Oh shit, was what I thought.

Jack Tyler started the car. 'Caplan is a major associate of some very dangerous criminals. We have had him under investigation for a year,' he says while doing a three-point turn.

'Twelve months is a long time. Why haven't you arrested him yet?'

'The person he works for never uses the same mule twice.'

'What do you mean?'

'A mule is someone who delivers merchandise, and collects payment for a third or fourth party.'

'Are you saying I'm a mule?' I said indignantly.

'Yes, you are without realising it. As I said, Caplan is connected to a very intelligent and dangerous criminal. I'm the third officer to be assigned to this case. The other two have had unfortunate accidents. These criminals have contacts in Africa, South America and the Middle East. They deal mainly in diamonds, but antiquities, art, gold, you name it. If it's coming into a country illegally or leaving, you can bet they have had a hand in it. I'm afraid you and your husband are involved with people who won't think twice about having you both disappear if it suits them.'

'Mark told me everything was in order. He has paperwork to prove it.'

'I've checked, and no documentation has been issued by the Kimberley Process Department regarding the transportation of diamonds for the past six months. So, the paperwork Mr Anderson has isn't official.' Silently, Tyler drove back along the narrow track.

At last, Vivien could see the bright lights of a road not far ahead.

'Mrs Anderson, did you open the envelope?'

'Yes,' I said,' thinking honesty would be the best policy now.

'What was in it, a key and an address perhaps?'

'How did you know?'

Jack Tyler shook his head, and then glanced in my direction. 'Will you help me bring these villains to account?' He asked quietly.

'What, and have an unfortunate accident in the process, I don't think so. Which reminds me, my husband was involved in a hit and run earlier today, do you think it was deliberate?'

Jack Tyler gave a non-committal shrug. 'Will you at least think about it?' he insisted.

As we sped back to the city I lay back against the headrest and closed my eyes, and remembered where I'd seen him before.

Tyler parked his rented Fiat in the car park at the back of the Hotel. He got out and walked around to the passenger side and offered his hand to assist me. The lighting wasn't good and I didn't recognise my hotel's surroundings. 'I don't think this is my hotel,' I told him.'

'It isn't. I thought you might want to get yourself cleaned up before returning to your husband.'

I doubted it was the real reason for bringing me here, but I didn't say. I was concerned though. 'Do Customs and Excise encourage you to kidnap people?' I asked him.

'Don't be an idiot, and just so you know, if you make a scene going through the lobby I'll arrest you there and then. There will be no second chances so think on.' Tyler took my arm and propelled me towards the double doors.

A sign with the name Caravaggio in large bold letters above the door made me smile. The irony of it, I thought. We walked to a reception desk where Tyler picked up his room key. An elevator took us up to the third floor and Tyler's room was located on the left, halfway down a corridor. I quickly made a mental note of these details in case I got the chance to make a run for it.

The hotel room consisted of a small double ornate walnut bed. The bedspread matched plain coral coloured curtains hanging each side of the small window. It was too dark outside to see any view there might have been, and I wondered if it led to a fire escape. A pair of still life paintings of fruit hung low on each side of the headboard. Tyler switched on lamps placed on tables on either side of the bed, the glow picked out colours in the fruit. The only other items of furniture were an armchair, a wardrobe and a matching chest of drawers, all in the same elaborate design as the bed.

'The bathrooms through there,' Tyler pointed to a door beside the wardrobe. 'While you're getting cleaned up, I'll order us some food. By the way, when you're undressed pass me your clothes and I'll get them laundered.'

'There's no need, they're not that bad.' I looked down at my black trousers and attempted to brush away smudges of dirt. I desperately wanted a shower though and couldn't bear the thought of having to put soiled clothes back on. I suspected Tyler wanted my clothes for another reason and to pacify him I agreed.

In the bathroom, I began to undress. I felt stiff and sore and I winced when I touched gravel graze near my elbow. I placed my clothes on a stool and slipped on the thick towelling robe that the hotel provided, and then stood at the door holding out my trousers, tee shirt and cardigan.

'What about the rest?' he asked impatiently.

'My bra and knickers are quite clean, thank you.' I told him, closing the door in his face.

I stood in the shower and let hot water cleanse away the day's ordeal. Through the clear glass of the shower door, I could see my bra hanging on the doorknob. Inside, pinned to the thin lining was the key Caplan had given me.

Twenty minutes later and dry, I dressed in the towelling robe again and wrapped a towel around my wet hair. Sandwiches, crisps and coffee were on a low table with Tyler sat in the armchair waiting for me. Suddenly conscious of how hungry I was I picked up a plate and piled it up.

'You'll have to stay here tonight.' Tyler told me after we'd finished eating. He put the used crockery back on the tray and placed it in the corridor outside.

'I'm not staying here with you. Mark will be wondering where I am.'

'You don't have a choice. The laundry service operates overnight so your clothes won't be ready until tomorrow morning.'

I didn't relish going back to our hotel, not yet anyway. I imagined the barrage of questions Mark would fire at me. The outrage my answers would cause. Staying here in Jack Tyler's hotel room would put off the inevitable and give me time to think. I sat on the bed and tucked my feet up, and then feigning exhaustion I lay back against the pillows. 'Where will you sleep, then? Were you able to acquire another room?' I asked, making it clear that as I was forced to spend the night, it wasn't going to be with him. I propped up the pillows and stretched out to also prove I wasn't about to give up the bed.

'I'll be sleeping in my hotel room, this one and in that bed, where else. You can take the armchair,' Tyler replied.

Without realising it, the belt from the robe I was wearing had worked loose and my cleavage and part of my right leg had made an appearance. I became aware of this when I saw Tyler's eyes travel the length of my body and hover over my thigh like a mosquito ready to dive. I pulled the robe closed quickly and he met my glare with a cheeky grin. 'A gentleman would take the armchair,' I said.

'Who said I was a gentleman? Don't worry, I'll sleep on top of the duvet and I promise I won't touch you.' Tyler held up his hands in mock surrender as he spoke.

'Oh,' I replied, wondering why I didn't feel reassured by this knowledge. I didn't feel afraid of him anymore and knew he didn't intend to hurt me. Information was all he wanted from me. I studied him as he undressed down to his boxers, impressed by his tall muscular body, smooth lightly tanned skin and black hair greying slightly at the temples. I suddenly felt like I might be missing out on something and had the urge to reach out and touch him. It disturbed me. Careful to keep my back to him I slipped off the robe and slid my naked body under the duvet. I had already discarded the towel around my hair.

After a moment I felt the bed dip as Jack lay down beside me and I listened to his rhythmic breathing. I was certain he wasn't asleep and after a few minutes, I slowly turned to face him and saw that I was right. 'Can't you sleep either?' I asked.

Intelligent green eyes met mine, and he looked at me, enquiringly.

'Who told you, you weren't any good at sex,' he said softly.

'Who do you think?' I replied, annoyed that he'd brought the subject up.

'Perhaps he's the one at fault.' As he spoke he lifted a strand of damp hair away from my face.

I closed my eyes. What was he implying? Suddenly the mattress moved again and when I opened my eyes I saw that he was about to get under the duvet.

'Excuse me, what do you think you're doing?' I asked, shocked at the audacity of the man. I flattened the duvet down in the middle to make a barrier so he couldn't get near me.

'It's cold in here and I just need to warm up a bit. Do you mind?'

Mr Tyler didn't give me time to object. While he'd been talking he'd unashamedly climbed into bed beside me. I could smell his woody aftershave again and feel the heat of his body and the nearness of him. I didn't like the look in his eye or his sudden embarrassed smile. Though, if I was being truthful I did like it. I told myself not to be ridiculous. What did I have to offer a man like Mr Tyler? Over the years Mark had shredded away all my self-esteem and I believed without a doubt that I wasn't good enough for him, or anyone else.

'What did you mean when you said, perhaps it was his fault?' I asked, pulling the top of the duvet up to my chin.

'Have you ever heard the expression, a bad workman blames his tools?'

I wasn't about to get into a discussion about men and their tools, a metaphor suggesting Mark lacked the ability or the equipment to perform, which wasn't true. If Mr Tyler assumed I was naïve, and I was certain he did, I decided to live up to his expectation and replied. 'Yes, but I don't understand what that has to do with anything.'

'In my experience, it's essential for some women to feel cherished and loved, for them to express their sexual preferences intimately and enjoy sex. Of course, not all women, or men, would agree with me.'

'You said some women.' I said.

'Yes, now how about we relax and keep each other warm.' The dent in the duvet lifted creating an affectionate haven.

'Are you married?' I felt compelled to ask.

'No.'

We studied each other for a few moments and then he leaned towards me. His kiss was persistent, lips soft on mine, his tongue gently exploring. When at last he released me, I knew he'd become aroused and wanted more.

'I think I will take the armchair, after all,' I told him, rising from the bed. I slipped on the towelling robe again and stood at the end of the bed hesitating, waiting. Was I hoping he would try and persuade me to get back into bed with him? What would I do if he did?

'You'll find a blanket and pillows on top of the wardrobe.' Mr Tyler mumbled, and it wasn't long before I heard the rhythmic breathing of a sleeping man.

The following morning when I opened my eyes it took me a minute to remember why I was sprawled in an armchair in a bedroom that wasn't in my hotel. I remembered and looked at the empty bed. The wardrobe was empty too, and Mr Tyler's suitcase was gone. Then I saw my brassiere on the floor. The sight of it kick-started me into movement and I picked up my bra knowing what I would find before I looked, or wouldn't find which was more than likely. Expecting to find the inside of my brassiere in shreds, I was surprised to find it wasn't. In place of the key Jack Tyler had pinned a note inside: THANK YOU.

'How could I have been such a fool,' was like a mantra I couldn't stop saying. I'd left my bra hanging on the bathroom door handle with the key inside waiting for him to find and steal it. I looked around for the rest of my clothes and remembered they were away being laundered. Mr Tyler had thought it all through. Had I woken earlier and seen what he was up to, he'd made sure I couldn't leave the hotel and follow him. Something occurred to me, a glimmer of hope. I lifted the internal telephone and dialled nine to the reception.

'Accoglienza come posso aiutare? Reception how can I help?'

'Hello, please could you check if Mr Tyler is in the restaurant having breakfast.'

'Mr Tyler prenotaro fuori dell 'hotel circa un'ora fa, e quella stanza ha bisogno di essere entro le ore 10.'

'Can you speak English, please?' I shouted, my hackles rising. I know it wasn't this man's fault but who else could I take my distress out on.

'Yes, of course. Mr Tyler booked out of the hotel an hour ago, and your room needs to be vacated by ten a.m.'

'Mr Tyler sent my clothes to be laundered and I'm waiting for them to be returned. I can't leave until I have clothes to wear, can I? Would you hurry them up, please?' I replaced the receiver and sat down on the bed and let the tears fall.

Twenty minutes later my clothes arrived. I dressed and went down for breakfast. I didn't care that I hadn't paid for the bed and breakfast room and I gave the waiter my sunniest smile while he poured coffee and looked at me suspiciously. I helped myself to the breakfast buffet and then left and started the long walk back to my hotel. I didn't have anything to give Mark, no painting, not even a key. I had nothing, except a number and an address.

CHAPTER 9

When Vivien arrived back at Hotel Muscatello she asked at reception for Helena and was told it was her day off. She checked the day's itinerary and saw that today they were free to do as they pleased. She asked at reception for a replacement key card to her room and as soon as she gave her name, the young man at the desk became apologetic. He explained to her in part Italian, part English that the police had been notified and security severely reprimanded. Nothing like it had ever happened before and he assured her nothing like it would happen again. Vivien looked back at him blankly. His name tag read Lorenzo and he seemed intelligent, but she didn't have the energy to get into a discussion she knew nothing about, so she nodded in the right places which seemed to satisfy him.

'We've upgraded you and your husband to a much superior room. You'll find a bottle of champagne and fruit as compensation and we hope you enjoy them, and the rest of your stay.' Lorenzo beamed a smile, accompanied by a deep sigh, giving Vivien the impression it was a relief to get it all off his chest.

Vivien took the elevator up to their new room. She hoped Mark had gone out and he had. A message on a scrap of paper and put on her pillow explained why.

Have an urgent business to attend to.
Get in touch with me on my mobile ASAP.
Mark

The number of Mark's mobile telephone number was stored in the Contacts folder of her iPhone which had been stolen along with her handbag. Vivien wasn't in a hurry to speak to him, so she freshened up, changed her clothes and then went back down to the reception desk.

Lorenzo looked pained to see her return so quickly. 'Is everything all right Signora?'

'Do you have my husband's mobile number, please?'

After a brief peruse of the computer, Lorenzo shook his head, 'no, Signora.'

Mark had involved Vivien in his criminal activity with no thought for her safety and subsequently, deliberately put her in danger. Jack Tyler hadn't had her answer to his request for help, and Mark's actions helped her to decide that she would. It depended on whether he still needed her, and as Vivien had the information he required she was sure he would be in touch sooner or later. Together they would bring Caplan to justice along with his accomplices, and that included Mark and Julie Merriton. She began walking in the direction of St. Peters square, remembering she'd previously seen side roads with independent shops and hoped that was where she would find a locksmith with key cutting facilities. At a road junction, she stopped to get her bearings. To her right, the River Tiber passed under a bridge. On the other side of the bridge was the towering cylindrical building of Castel Sant' Angelo, known as Hadrian's Tomb. By this time, Vivien desperately needed another coffee and she looked for a ristorante. She found one that looked inviting and sat at a corner table away from the window. Inside was smoky and she guessed it was mostly frequented by locals. Three men sat by the window playing a card game, they gave her a cursory glance as she entered then ignored her and went back to their game.

The key Caplan had given her wasn't big. It resembled the locker key she used when she went swimming at the Northgate Area baths in Chester City, but slightly larger. Earlier, while in their hotel room she'd made a quick search and found the keys to Lilac House in one of the bedside tables. Vivien took them out of the small bag she had brought with her. She'd packed this additional bag to use with her evening wear for dinner at the hotel. In the light of day, the black satin clutch with a gold chain looked incongruous placed on the red and white check plastic tablecloth. With her other handbag stolen this was what she'd had to use. One of the keys among the bundle was of a similar size and shape to the key Caplan had given her, and Jack had stolen. It was just what she needed. At home, it opened a large filing cabinet in the office in which Mark kept all his receipts and insurance documents, and goodness knew what else. Anyway, Vivien decided it would fit the bill for the new key.

The ristorante proprietor directed Vivien to a locksmith a few streets away and luckily he was open for business and she managed to get the duplicate done there and then. When Vivien exited the locksmiths a man on the other side of the street caught her attention. Probably because his leg was in bright blue plaster and he struggled to walk on crutches. Vivien thought of Mark and wondered how he was managing with his broken leg. It took her a moment to grasp that the man across the road was Mark. Vivien's first instinct was to wave to get his attention. After all, she thought naively, she had nothing to worry about now. He'll probably be annoyed the jeweller hadn't given her the money he needed to pay for the painting, but surely after she'd explained, and the key, he thought would open the locker was in his possession, all would be well. Vivien wasn't about to take that risk though. She didn't wave. Instead, she turned and went back inside the locksmith's shop and looked at house name plaques that were secured on one wall. The shopkeeper eyed her over the top of his spectacles with interest, envisaging further profit.

Vivien thought about following Mark. Perhaps she would glean some information useful to Jack Tyler. Vivien decided against it and began making her way back towards the bridge and her hotel.

Mark made slow progress and it took him a while to reach the ristorante where he had agreed to meet Antonio. It was a few doors away from the one that Vivien had vacated less than an hour ago. This one though was upmarket with clean blue cotton tablecloths and a flower in a bud vase alongside the condiments. Mark assumed Antonio was on his way and ordered a sandwich and a coffee for himself while he waited.

When Antonio finally sat down opposite Mark, he didn't bother with niceties but got straight to the point. 'Did you find Vivien?' he asked.

'No, she wasn't at the hotel when I returned.' The waiter brought another coffee and placed it in front of Antonio. The bill, a small square of paper on a plate, he placed in front of Mark.

'What about Jack Tyler? What time did you arrange to meet him here?'

'I haven't been able to get hold of him.' Mark knew it best not to mention he'd thought better of it and hadn't tried. It was bad enough knowing the customs and excise were on his case, without getting mixed up in whatever Antonio had in mind for Mr Tyler.

'We have a problem then, don't we?' Antonio said.

'Vivien will show up soon, I'm sure. After all, where else would she go if not back to our hotel?' Mark attempted to reassure Antonio whose expression conveyed nothing but disapproval.

Antonio stirred sugar into his coffee and took a sip. 'I meant Jack Tyler. Also beside him and your wife we have another problem. On further inspection, the jeweller, Caplan, has realised that the diamonds aren't worth the amount he's paid for them. He wants a further twenty thousand pounds worth of uncut diamonds to make up the shortfall.'

'You'll have to speak to Julie about that. I paid her my share for the painting, and it was she who purchased the diamonds. I'm not responsible if some have turned out to be poor quality.'

'Caplan isn't someone you mess around with, nor is my boss, so you'll pay.' The irritation in Antonio's voice was palpable. 'You're getting a genuine Caravaggio, remember, and worth far more than you are paying.'

'It's worth nothing until validated. Although I have to admit, I'm ninety-nine per cent sure that the painting you showed me is the genuine article.' Mark said.

'Yes and as I've already told you, it will have a certificate to prove it.'

'I want to meet your expert and be there when he inspects it and gives his opinion. Don't take me for a complete fool, Antonio.'

'That may not be possible but I will do my best. First, you need to prioritise finding your wife and getting the key, or you'll get nothing.'

'I don't understand why you and Julie needed me in the first place. You needed someone to bring the diamonds to Rome, I realise that. Although even that doesn't make sense, according to Julie it isn't against the law to take rough diamonds out of the UK and into Italy. Not while we're still in the EU. I could have handed them to you on that first day when we met. You could have taken the diamonds to the jeweller? You would have the key by now and the money for the painting. Why all the subterfuge, I don't understand?'

'Would you have handed the diamonds over to me, just like that, I don't think so. You hardly trust me now. Also, the customs and excise investigator, Jack Tyler, is watching my every move. We needed a third party. You're the one purchasing the painting and you had already arranged a visit to Rome. It was convenient for us to do it this way. You were unknown in Rome. Unfortunately for you, you're not any longer.'

Mark arrived back at Hotel Muscatello to find Vivien waiting for him. He was so relieved to see her that he laid his crutches down on the bed and hugged her. 'Are you alright,' he asked. 'I heard what happened, were you hurt?'

His concern seemed genuine and it took Vivien by surprise. 'I'm fine, just a few grazes and this bump on my head.' She lifted her hand and gingerly touched the sore spot.

'Well, I had to spend the night in the hospital. When I came back to the hotel our room had been ransacked. I'm going to claim compensation for the inconvenience.'

'Yes, the man on reception explained.' Vivien had expected him to ask where she'd spent the previous night. To be interested in Caplan and what he said, and what had happened to her after the mugging, but her rehearsed replies were unnecessary.

'Have you got the key, Caplan gave you. I need to get it to Antonio as soon as possible.' Concern and affection over, Mark, as usual, was too self-absorbed to care about what had happened to his wife.

Vivien opened her bag and pulled out the key she'd had made. 'Here it is,' she said and handed it to Mark. She also gave him a scrap of paper. On it, she had written the address where the locker could be found and a number.

'Brilliant,' Mark snatched them from her and immediately telephoned Antonio to give him the good news.

CARAVAGGIO IN THE CITIES OF MILAN AND ROME

1589/1606

At the end of the apprenticeship in 1589, Caravaggio stayed in Milan. For his protection, Caravaggio became an excellent swordsman. He was fearless, belligerent, and soon feared by many. At the age of twenty-one, Caravaggio travelled from Milan to Rome where he struggled to find decent lodgings and settle. He found jobs as a copyist and a painter of fruit and flowers. The money he made was insufficient to live on and his small inheritance soon ran out. Caravaggio realised he needed to acquire a protector and began to search one out. Around this time a man named Bernardino became his friend and Caravaggio painted his portrait in 1593. Bernardino Cersari was the brother of Cavalier d'Arpino and Caravaggio began working for him around this time. The position he held in the flourishing studio meant that at last, he had gained a foothold in the Roman art world. He grew into a tall large young man. He wore his black beard thin and his mass of black curly hair hung low over his forehead, and his hooded black eyes looked out under bushy eyebrows. He wore only black which suited the mood he was generally in. He was central to the band of artists that had befriended him but he could be hostile. Caravaggio was quick to respond to an offence, or in defence of his honour and reputation.

Caravaggio painted fast and he produced a remarkable number of works from these years. A memory from his student years regularly surfaced. He embellished the scene using shadowy backgrounds on his canvases with his subjects positioned in shafts of light.

While living in Rome his life became increasingly stormy. He argued with a well-known Roman Pimp, Ranuccio Tomassoni which resulted in a sword fight. During the fight, Caravaggio aimed his sword at Tomassoni's thigh or groin, but the blade stabbed him higher and Tomassoni was gravely injured in the stomach. Caravaggio too was badly wounded. He could do nothing but watch as Tomassoni lay bleeding to death.

Accused of murder and to avoid capture Caravaggio fled to Palestrina and lived under the protection of the Colonna family who was beyond the range of papal jurisdiction. Later Caravaggio moved on to Naples.

CHAPTER 10

Early the following morning Antonio paced Hotel Muscatello's lobby waiting for Mark. The lift door had already shuddered open three times spilling out visitors on their way out but as yet no sign of Mark. Seated at a small round table in a corner two men sat, also waiting. Antonio was angered by their presence. Matteo and Stefano were his father's bodyguards, men employed by Alonzo to sort out problems, tie up loose ends and clear up any mess resulting from it. Matteo, the larger man, sat staring in Antonio's direction, a clear attempt to intimidate him. It didn't work. No matter if Antonio fell short of his father's expectations, Alonzo would never give these men instructions for his son to be harmed. Stefano, the smaller of the two and slim compared to his companion was just as muscular but wiry and faster. He leafed through a magazine seemingly bored.

It upset Antonio to discover his father didn't trust him to see the deal through to completion. It didn't help to know that it was his fault. He'd stupidly made the mistake of telling Alonzo about Jack Tyler questioning Mark, and that Vivien Anderson had delivered the diamonds to Caplan, instead of her husband as arranged. Even so, if his father had been patient a little longer, there would have been no need to send his bullies.

The lift doors opened and again visitors piled out. This time they included Mark, who made his way awkwardly on his crutches towards Antonio. Matteo and Stefano stood and walked over to join them. Matteo towered over Mark who looked at Antonio questioningly.

Before Antonio had a chance to introduce Mark to his father's men, Matteo spoke. 'Give me the key,' he growled, holding out a large beefy hand.

Taken aback, Mark hesitated. He looked from one to the other and then directing his words to Antonio, he said. 'What's going on?'

'It's nothing to worry about. They're here to act as bodyguards, due to the amount of money I'll be collecting.' Antonio attempted to reassure Mark. He glared at Matteo and said. 'Back off.'

'Before I hand anything over, I believe you have a key for me in exchange, don't you?'

Antonio withdrew a small key out of his pocket and handed it to Mark, attached to it was a locker number. Happy, at last, Mark placed the key Vivien had given him into Antonio's hand and glared at Matteo in defiance.

'We will take you to the Rail terminal now and complete the deal to everyone's satisfaction,' Antonio said, smiling at Matteo and Stefano in triumph.

Vivien hadn't slept well and was astounded when she woke to find it was already nine a.m. She took a long hot shower, dressed and dried her hair and then applied a little makeup and lipstick. She didn't intend to go anywhere but it made her feel better. She rang reception for room service and sat worried about what would happen when Antonio found out the key he'd been given was a dud. Thirty minutes later a knock on the door made her jump. She stood with her hand on the door handle but didn't open it. Could it be Mark? Had Antonio found out so soon that he'd been duped? The knock came again, and she heard a voice outside saying her name.

Vivien plucked up courage and opened the door and came face to face with Jack Tyler. He didn't speak to her but pushed past with a laden breakfast trolley.

'Your breakfast, Signora,' he said, with a mock salute and then began uncovering the plates of food.

Vivien stayed by the door. 'Thank you, I'll leave a tip for the staff before I leave.'

Tyler smiled, 'Hi Vivien.'

Vivien didn't answer. Now that he was here standing in front of her, all she could do was look at him. He'd dressed in a lightweight pale grey suit, the sort Mark favoured, but on Jack, it fitted perfectly. He wasn't wearing a tie and had left the top three buttons of his pale blue shirt open. Vivien couldn't take her eyes away from the hollow at the base of his neck. Everything about him glowed. The soft waves in his hair, smooth tanned skin, all invited her touch. She should be angry with him, but couldn't be.

While Vivien stood looking at Tyler he had decided to help himself to toast and marmalade. He waved her over as he munched away. 'Come and have some breakfast, we'll talk afterwards.'

'I'm not sure I have anything to say to you.' Vivien retorted, then walked over and sat on the edge of the bed.

'You do, you just haven't decided what not to tell me.' Tyler poured coffee for them both.

Vivien relented and began to eat. Having Tyler beside her had given her an appetite, and she knew it wasn't just for food. After a few mouthfuls, she said. 'You could have asked me for the key. You didn't have to steal it. I would have given it to you, eventually. What you did was unkind. Leaving me in the hotel without saying goodbye, especially after what happened.'

'What happened?'

'You don't remember?' Vivien looked at him appalled. She had relived their kiss so many times and yet clearly it had meant nothing to him.

'With Mark, when you got back to the hotel.'

'Oh!' Vivien resented Jack's blasé attitude. He was all customs and excise officer now, intent only on pumping her for information. Vivien stood and walked over to the window. The view from her hotel was over the red and brown tiled roofs of the hotels and houses surrounding Piazza Navona. She wished she was there right now having coffee in one of the pretty cafes, instead of here with this chauvinistic man. Pigeons cooed on the window ledge and she swished the curtain to shoo them away.

Tyler was watching her. 'Well,' he said.

'Stop interrogating me, or leave, you're good at that.'

'So the key I took from inside your dainty bra was the one Caplan gave you?'

'Yes, I told you.'

'It's a locker key, although I don't know what it opens yet.'

'You should have stopped to ask me before stealing it.' Vivien replied resentfully.

'Never mind about that now, I've just seen your husband and Antonio exchange keys, presumably to finalise the deal. I don't understand why there's a third key. Come on, Vivien, explain.'

'Why do you think? This mix up is your entire fault. When you stole the key from me I had nothing to give Mark. You can only imagine what his reaction would have been if I'd turned up empty-handed. So I had a duplicate made of the key to our filing cabinet, back in Woodbury.'

'What the hell were you thinking? You do know that you've put Mark in great danger, don't you?' Tyler was quiet for a moment. 'I have the correct key to the locker containing the money, payment for the painting, right? You have the receipt and information for where the locker is, so it will save a lot of trouble if you just give that to me, and I'll be on my way. If I'm to sort this and make sure no harm comes to Mark, I need to act quickly.'

'I flushed the receipt down Caplan's toilet.'

'You did what?'

'After I had memorised what I needed to know.'

Jack let out a breath. 'I see, and can you still remember it.'

'Yes, of course.'

'Good, you're coming with me then.' Jack grabbed Vivien's hand and began pulling her towards the door.

'Where are we going?'

'You tell me.'

Vivien just had time to grab her jacket and slip a lipstick into the pocket before Jack frogmarched her out of the room.

CHAPTER 11

Vivien

Tyler was correct in thinking that the receipt Caplan had given me was for a luggage locker. It was at the Rail Terminal, at Piazza Dei Cinquecento. I gave him the address and he drove us straight there. We parked the car on a side street not far from the Terminal and walked the rest of the way. On the first floor, we found a restaurant and snack bar and Jack bought two cappuccinos. I needed the toilet so I left him and walked the length of the terminal looking for a Ladies' sign. I passed a stall selling handbags and suitcases and stopped to browse, tempted to replace the one I'd had stolen. On the way back, I gave in and bought a medium-sized rucksack, black with green trim. The vastness of the terminal surprised me. Everywhere tourists and locals queued for tickets while rail personnel meandered about. When I returned to the lounge, Tyler had already finished his drink and as soon as he saw me he stood.

'I'll go to the locker now while you drink your coffee, and I'll see you back here in about fifteen minutes. What's the number?' Jack looked at me impatiently while I took a sip.

'I'm coming with you,' I told him and quickly finished my now lukewarm drink.

The Baggage Storage was located a few steps from the Terminal's main entrance. It took a few minutes to explain to the customer service person that we had lost the receipt. Thankfully Tyler spoke fluent Italian and with his charm and good looks he soon had the woman eager to help. All the lockers were situated in alcoves off long corridors, in stacks of three, one on top of the other. The locker we wanted was at the bottom. Jack opened it and we both crouched down to see inside. A large holdall filled the space and when Jack opened it I saw bundles of paper Euros inside filling the holdall to the brim.

Tyler smiled at me as he zipped up the holdall again. He stood with it safely in his hand. 'Thank you, Vivien,' he said. He raised his arm and cupped the back of my head in his hand and then leaned towards me and brushed my cheek with his lips.

'What now?' I asked when we'd arrived back in the lounge area.

'Sit and wait here for ten minutes and then make your way to the ground floor and stand near the exit. I won't be long.' Before I had time to respond Tyler disappeared into the crowd, the bag full of money still in his hand.

I sat wondering if history would repeat itself and he'd run out on me again. I made my way to the ground floor and waited for him a few metres from the exit. I heard a voice say my name and I turned to see Mark leaning heavily on his crutches by my side. A cardboard tube was tucked under his armpit.

'Vivien, what are you doing here?' he asked. He looked pale and in pain, and perspiring heavily.

'I worried about how you were managing on your crutches so I came to see if I could help.' I had to think quickly, so I lied. I looked in the direction I thought Jack Tyler might appear hoping he didn't decide to return just then.

'I'm pleased to say all went well, Vivien, and I have my Caravaggio at last.' Mark looked pleased and he beamed at me. 'I am struggling though, especially having to carry it around with me. Will you take it? I took the cardboard tube containing the painting from him and relaxed a little.

'Come on then, don't dawdle, we need to get it safely back to our hotel room and quickly.' Mark began manoeuvring his way through the crowds towards the exit doors and I followed. We'd almost reached them when I remembered my new rucksack. I'd placed it on a chair while I waited for Jack. Mark gave me his usual exasperated look. 'I'll hail a taxi while you get it, but hurry up,' he demanded.

Thankfully the bag was still there. I tucked in the cardboard tube and hurried back to catch up with Mark. I'd reached the exit again and stopped. A large black car screeched to a halt at the pavement kerb where Mark stood. Antonio was in the driving seat and I could see him shouting instructions to two men in the car with him. Both men exited the car and the shorter, more agile of the two grabbed Mark's crutches and threw them into the boot. He stood looking around at the crowds outside the terminal, hyped up, his body tense. He looked towards the exit doors and I saw his eyes narrow. The larger man had pushed Mark into the back seat and was sat beside him. I stood helpless not knowing what I should do when suddenly, a hand grabbed my arm and began pulling me backwards.

It was Jack Tyler, he'd come back. He must have witnessed Mark's abduction because I heard him on his mobile asking for Berardi, and then convey what had happened. After ending the call he glanced outside and I did the same. The car with Mark in it had gone. The shorter man was walking towards the exit doors, coming straight at us.

'Never a dull moment with you, is there?' Tyler said, taking off in the direction of the nearest platform, me at his heels. The platform had train tracks in rows of two straight lines. They speared to the left and right and then

103

disappeared into the distance. On the far side, a waiting train was silent, and passengers stood in groups ready to board it.

My jogging turned into a fast walk as I tried to catch my breath. I was a few metres behind Jack who looked to be heading towards the end of the platform. I called to him, 'Hold on a minute,' and he slowed down a little.

'You can rest soon, come on.' The end of the platform stopped abruptly and we stood teetering on the edge with nowhere else to go. A metal door in a narrow alcove was on our right and Tyler tried the handle. Thankfully it opened and we dodged through and out of sight. The area we found ourselves in was windowless and dark. Tyler flipped a switch and an overhead electric strip light lit the room. Cardboard boxes and shelves full of plastic cartons filled the area, an obvious storeroom for the restaurant. 'We should be alright in here for a moment,' he said, leaning against the back of the door.

'Where are those men taking, Mark,' I asked, as soon as my breathing returned to normal.

'I wouldn't like to say but can hazard a guess.'

Tyler didn't elaborate and I didn't probe. I had the sense it was best not to know. Tyler had told me I was playing a precarious game but I didn't care. In the last forty-eight hours I had lived another life and had never felt more alive. 'Between us, we have the money and the painting,' I told Tyler and he frowned at me. I pulled the top of my rucksack open and showed him what was inside.

'You never fail to surprise me, Mrs Anderson.'

'I'll take that as a compliment.'

'There's nothing we can do to help Mark. The police have it in hand, so I suggest you go back to your hotel and wait for news. I'll put the money and painting somewhere safe back in my hotel.'

Jack reached for the painting and I sensed rather than

saw him suddenly tense. He put a finger to his lips to shut me up as he placed his foot against the door bracing his shoulder against it to stop it from opening. The door handle turned and gave a slight squeak. We both stood listening, me holding my breath. After a moment Jack relaxed. He started walking towards the nearest pile of cardboard boxes and he beckoned me to follow. A narrow space had been left between the stacks and we weaved our way through. The storeroom was larger than it looked but at last, at the far end, I saw a half-glazed door. Through it, a bright light shone and Tyler peered through.

'This is a staff door leading into a kitchen to one of the ground floor cafes. We're going to have to make a run for the car. It might be better if I go alone, I'll be quicker.'

'I don't like the sound of that,' I told him.

'It will be fine. Wait here for a few minutes and then start walking through. You'll come out near the main exit doors but don't head for there. Turn right and go towards the Baggage Storage Counter. I'll be in my car waiting for you near there. Now, give me the painting.' Reluctantly I handed my rucksack to him.

Five minutes later I did as Jack had instructed.

'Non dovresti essere qui,' a cook shouted at me as I hurried past him. A tall white hat wobbled above his head.

'Sorry, non-parlo la lingua.' I replied, smiling.

As soon as I was back in the rail terminal's main walkway I was tempted to run but I knew my life might depend on not drawing attention to myself. I reached the Baggage Storage and looked around for Jack. The area was pedestrianised and so nowhere for Jack to bring his car. Jack had the money and the painting now. The thought that I had been taken in again surfaced? After all, what did I know about him? Was he really who he said he was. Passports can be forged. Identity fraud is rampant. I began to panic.

I noticed cars going past on a road at the end of the rail terminal building. Trying to avoid the queues and small mounds of suitcases I walked as quickly as I could towards it and then peered around the corner. I almost burst into tears because there was Jack in his car patiently waiting for me. He flashed the car headlights once and I ran towards him. I heard a shout behind me but I didn't look back. Jack had the car door open and the engine revving. I jumped in beside him and we sped off.

The man who'd been searching for us stood on the pavement. He shook his fist and glared as we passed.

Fear, relief, excitement, or just plain stupidity, I don't know, but I burst out laughing. I looked at Jack Tyler so cool and calm and not laughing and my sides ached by the time I had my giggles under control.

'I want to see the painting, Mr Tyler. I think I deserve that, don't you? Maybe I could come back to your hotel and you can show me your etchings.' I gave him my best smile and tossed back my hair in a frivolous way. 'What do you say?'

Jack looked at me strangely. 'Come on then,' he said, 'if you insist.'

Jack stopped on the way and bought a bottle of wine which he opened and poured us both a drink as soon as we entered his room. It was a different hotel but the layout pretty much the same as the previous one.

'Right then, let's see what all the fuss is about shall we?' Jack put the thick cardboard tube on the bed and carefully took out the painting. He opened it out flat on the bedspread. As soon as he let go, the canvas rolled closed so we both stood on either side with a finger on each corner to keep it open. I looked at the painting and immediately understood Mark's obsession with the painter. This was what Mark had risked our lives for.

The painting is of a dark-haired young boy holding a sharp knife. There is fruit on a table and he is peeling a nectarine. His right arm rests on what looks like a plaited rug thrown over the back of a chair. Although his eyes are downcast, there is a sense of pleasure in the task, a slight lift to the corners of his lips as though in anticipation of the taste to come.

'This looks like a genuine Caravaggio,' I said. 'The skin tone, colour and texture of the fruit are perfect. Is there a certificate with it?'

Tyler rolled the painting back up again. 'Signed slips of paper mean nothing coming from the likes of the Cortez family. I'll organise to have it properly authenticated once I get back to my office in Manchester.' Suddenly he turned to me and took me in his arms. He kissed me long and lingering and I felt my insides slide in all directions. He gave my bottom an affectionate tap. 'You've seen my etchings now let's get down to business.'

'What do you mean?'

'Don't be coy, Vivien. It's what we both want, isn't it?'

'Don't get your hopes up, Mr Tyler. I meant it when I said I'm not very good at sex. I think I might be frigid.' I was embarrassed by my confession and couldn't look at him. The thought of his distaste was unbearable.

'I'll be the judge of that.' Tyler replied, adding, 'Please call me Jack.'

'Let's take a shower together first,' I suggested, stalling for time. 'You go ahead and get the water lovely and hot. I'll be with you in a minute.' I began to undress and Jack grinned at me in the boyish way he had, and then he walked into the bathroom. Quickly I picked up the painting and carefully put it back into my rucksack. For it to be hidden completely I had to bend the top edges slightly. I trusted I hadn't done any more damage than may be time and dry conditions had already inflicted on it. The empty cardboard tube lay on the sideboard and I hoped Jack wouldn't realise the painting was missing from inside until he was back in Manchester.

When at last Jack kissed me again, his lips moved soft and urgent against mine. All thoughts of Mark, Caplan, the key, even Isobel fled from my mind, and I gave myself up to him completely. My need became urgent and I let his fingers explore my private places and enjoyed the sensation he aroused within me. His lips caressed my nipples, and other places, stirring the very core of me. When at last he entered me I groaned with a desire I had never known before. We moved as one in a satisfying rhythm, and then more urgently until I lost all control and my body moved of its own accord. I shrieked in pleasure at the moment of climax and we both burst into a fit of laughing.

'I can honestly say that you are not frigid, Vivien.' Jack told me before we fell asleep wrapped in each other's arms. Like two spoons we curled up in the large bed and satiated we slept away the rest of the afternoon. I woke first and lay facing him watching him sleep, listening to his breathing and the slight nasal noises he made. I rose slowly from the bed and began to dress. Before I left with the painting, I wrote a short note and left it for him on the pillow beside him: *THANK YOU.*

It was something I thought he might appreciate.

Outside the hotel, I tried to get my bearings. Jack had raced me off to the rail terminal earlier, not giving me a chance to get my clutch bag. I didn't have my street map with me so I wasn't sure how far away from Hotel Muscatello I was. I knew I couldn't get lost though, and besides Taxi's were in plenty of supply and easy to hail. I decided to start walking. Hadrian's Mausoleum was a landmark easily seen and so I made that my focal point to aim for. Once there, it was just a matter of crossing St Angelo's bridge and follow the street directions to Piazza Navona.

I hadn't gone far when an overwhelming sadness gripped me. The warmth and gentleness I had experienced with Jack were like an epiphany. A sudden insight into what I'd missed all the years married to Mark. Tears streamed down my face unheeded, silent, without a sob or cry of anguish. I found a bench and let my grief wash over me. I sat with the rucksack on my knees wondering what had possessed me to take the painting. Would Jack get into trouble for losing it? Is that what I want, why I did it? I'd burnt my bridges with him now, hadn't I? Once he realised what I'd done, there would be no going back.

CHAPTER 12

Antonio drove his father's black Range Rover out of the main bustle of the city. He headed for Ponte Casilino and it wasn't long before the road signs came into view.

Mark also saw the signs and remembered this was where the jeweller lived. He was sat in the back of the car next to Matteo, too afraid to speak. He'd tried it after being pushed into the car and had demanded an explanation. In reply, he'd received a brutal punch to the side of his face which had broken two of his teeth. His mouth had filled with blood and the taste of it made him gag. He'd coughed and spat out a glob staining his shirt and jacket. Matteo sat glaring at him in disgust, his big fisted hands in his lap, knuckles smeared with Mark's blood. Mark knew Vivien was responsible for the mess he was now in. He'd made the mistake of trusting her to do a simple job, to deliver the diamonds and get the payment. He cursed her silently, promising to make his stupid bitch of a wife pay.

Arriving at the destination Antonio parked the car beside a line of garages underneath a block of apartments. Matteo brought the crutches from the boot and then pulled Mark out of the car and propelled him towards the last garage in the row. Antonio lifted the up and over metal door and flicked on a light switch. As the garage door closed the naked glass bulb hanging from the ceiling cast dark shadows and elongated theirs. In the middle of the garage, an upright chair was placed.

Surrounding it and underneath were maroon coloured blotches staining the concrete. Mark tried to dismiss the thought that it was dried blood.

'Sit down, Mark.' Antonio commanded.

Mark shuffled over to the chair and sat. He desperately needed to pee and knew he couldn't hold it for much longer. Matteo secured Mark's feet to the front legs of the chair with tape, then bound his torso to the back of the chair and tied his wrists together. Mark knew it was useless to resist. Stay calm, he thought, knowing how impossible that was going to be.

Antonio stood behind Mark and began to speak. He sounded frustrated, not particularly angry, and Mark took some comfort in that. 'The locker number and the key you gave me proved useless. So, we still need the payment for the Caravaggio painting you collected, and you'll stay here until we get it. Do you understand?' Mark nodded. 'I'm going to get Vivien on the telephone now and you're going to tell her to bring the key or the money to me.' Antonio made the call to Hotel Muscatello.

'What if Vivien doesn't have the money,' Mark said. The words coming out of his beaten mouth sounded like, 'Wah if Vifin doth haf the mummy.' Antonio gave a slight nod to Matteo who obliged by punching Mark again, this time aiming for his left eye.

'Ciao Lorenzo, è Helena lì.' Antonio spoke into the mobile and then listened to the hotel's concierge, Lorenzo's, reply. After a few minutes and looking concerned, he ended the call and rang another number. He held a short conversation in Italian and then Mark heard Antonio cry out like a wounded animal. Antonio ended the call and spoke to Matteo in a voice full of pain and anguish.

Ignoring Mark, both men walked outside. Matteo flicked off the light and closed the garage door, leaving

Mark in the dark and alone.

Antonio sped out of Rome as fast as the speed limit would allow. Once on the outskirts and into country lanes, he stepped on the accelerator. Matteo sat beside him stony-faced wondering how the news would affect him.

The conversation with Helena earlier had left Antonio shaken and grief-stricken. After his father's heart health scare, the hospital had advised that he stay overnight. There were further tests that needed to be done. Helena had driven their mother and brother, Roberto home. Alina had been distressed with worry, and so his sister thought it wise to stay the night. The next morning when Helena called the hospital to enquire how her father was, she was assured he was quite well and itching to return home. Now his father was dead.

Antonio parked the car and ran up the few steps towards the open front door. He called out to his mother and rushed through the house looking for them. His family sat around the kitchen table grey-faced and with red-rimmed eyes.

'Where is he,' Antonio demanded.

'The ambulance left a short while ago, they have taken him away.' His mother stood and began sobbing and Antonio wrapped his arms around her.

'I want to see him.' Antonio told her.

'Yes, later. There is nothing we can do for him now.'

Antonio turned to his sister. 'Tell me what happened.'

'The first thing father did when we arrived home was to go to his studio.' Helena told him. 'Mother and I began to prepare lunch and about an hour later, when father hadn't come down, we sent Roberto up to fetch him. Poor Roberto found his father on the floor. He had suffered a massive heart attack, a real one this time. He passed away before the ambulance arrived. If only we hadn't been so concerned about food and checked on him earlier.'

'You mustn't blame yourself,' Antonio said, in an attempt to comfort her. 'Did he say anything before he died?'

'I think he tried to tell us something. He lay staring at the empty easel. He attempted to raise his arm to point at it, but couldn't manage it. The pain was too much for him. He loved the Caravaggio painting didn't he, Antonio?' Helena led the way up the stairs and into Alonzo's studio as she spoke.

'Where is it?' Antonio looked around. On his father's work table lay Alonzo's rendition of the painting, Boy Peeling Fruit. Antonio looked at the place on the floor where his father had laid pointing at the empty easel and he suddenly felt very sick.

CHAPTER 13

Mark shivered. It was cold in the garage and the temperature had dropped since they'd brought him there. He could only guess the time. There had been no sounds of voices outside, no cars pulling up to park. An occasional banging of a door roused him and he'd shouted for help a few times. Nobody came to his aid so he soon gave up. The smell of his pee offended him. The foot of his broken leg sticking out had escaped the urine, but his good foot sat in a puddle of it. His mouth was dry and he prayed to a God he didn't believe in for a drink. Whisky preferably, he pleaded. The recurring thought that Antonio might leave him here to die of thirst and starvation caused him to shake uncontrollably.

When the garage door finally lifted and Mark saw Matteo and Stefano he almost cried in relief. Stefano brought a bottle of water to his bloodied mouth and let Mark take a long swallow. 'Thank you,' he told Stefano gratefully.

Mark's joy was short-lived. Antonio had instructed the men to interrogate Mark and then clear up the mess. 'Make it look like another accident. Poor some whiskies down his throat, he'll like that, and it may make him more pliable. I need to know what he's done with the painting.'

Matteo was only too happy to oblige. Stefano looked on.

'Where is the Caravaggio painting you've taken from the locker?' Matteo shouted.

'I gave it to Vivien,' Mark answered truthfully.
'Why?'
'She was there, at the rail terminal. I was struggling with my crutches and she took it from me to help.'
'What was she doing there?'
'She told me she came looking for me.'
'Your wife lied. She was with a customs and excise officer, named Jack Tyler. She gave him the key to the locker containing the money. She's made a fool out of you.' Matteo looked at Stefano and they both sniggered.

'Made a fool out of you lot too, by the looks of it.' Mark regretted his outburst immediately. Matteo's fist connected to the side of Marks's head and everything around him went black.

When Mark woke he was in the back of a car again. It smelled of cigarettes and was littered with empty packets and sweet wrappers. The car pulled up near St Angelo's bridge and Stefano helped him out. The bridge was almost empty and the few Italians crossing it made sure to mind their own business and ignore the trio. At the top of the steps, Mark hesitated. Stefano had hold of his crutches and Mark looked at him in dismay.

'I can't get down there with my broken leg.'
'Yes, you can.' Matteo replied as he gave Mark a hard push.

Mark hit every sharp edge of the stone steps on his way down. He heard his good leg crack as a bone broke. His right arm twisted underneath him as he dropped onto the stone towpath, fractured in two places. Unable to move, he screamed out in pain.

Matteo and Stefano raced down the steps following Mark's descent. They lifted his broken legs and dragged him under the main arch of the bridge.

Stefano let whisky from a bottle sip down Mark's throat. 'This will help with the pain, Mr Anderson.' Mark gulped it down and Stefano poured in more.

St Angelo's bridge was almost empty when Vivien began to cross. Tourists were back in their hotels preparing for their evening meals or indulging in pre-dinner drinks. Halfway across the bridge, she spotted the two men who had abducted Mark. They had come up the stone steps from the river underneath the bridge and suddenly appeared in front of her. Vivien froze. There was nowhere to hide. Luckily the men turned and walked away in the opposite direction.

Vivien ran down the steps and looked around to see if Mark was there. She stood out of sight from above beside the stone support. The river looked like ink in the deep shadows, its depths fathomless. Gentle lapping licked at the bottom of three large stone arches supporting the bridge and road above. She could hear a few people on the bridge chatting as they crossed. It invaded the empty stillness of her surroundings and she was glad of it. Vivien kept to the inner edge of the towpath and listened and then took a few more steps underneath the bridge. She saw Mark and hurried over to where he lay.

Mark looked back at her from a bloodied face and a swollen eye. He groaned in pain and Vivien knelt beside him. She noticed how near to the towpath edge he was, inches from the river's swirling water. 'Keep still, it's best you don't move.'

'I know that,' Mark snapped back at her, his voice raw. 'Have you still got the painting, is it safe?'

'Yes quite safe.' Vivien assured him. She never bothered to mention that it was in her rucksack a few feet from where he lay, or that the money Antonio should have received was being looked after by a customs and excise officer. 'Will you be all right?'

Mark opened a bloodshot eye and glared at her. 'Do I

look all right?'

'I meant, all right on your own while I go for help.'

'Antonio said the key I'd given him was a dud, so where's the key Caplan gave you?' Mark moved in an attempt to face her and rolled closer to the water's edge. He cried out as broken bones jarred. 'Did you decide to double-cross me, Vivien? You won't get away with it, you'll pay don't worry. I'd kill you right now if I had the strength? Antonio's men have beaten me half to death because of you.' Mark tried to sit and began coughing. Vivien noticed blood in his mouth. 'Did you hear what I said?' Mark groaned and lay back down.

'Yes, and I'll explain everything to you later, but right now we need to get you to a hospital.' Vivien stood.

Mark began mumbling a jumble of words. His face was grey and greasy with sweat, his words incoherent. He noticed Vivien still by his side and cried out from his delirium. 'For God's sake go and get help, I'm dying here. Do something right for once in your life.'

'All right Mark.' Vivien looked at him sadly and after a few moments, she walked away.

Back in her hotel room, Vivien waited nervously. She wished Jack would get in touch with her, even if it was only to berate her. She wondered what he was doing now. There was so much she wanted to say, to tell him. The word sorry was a major part of it. She took a shower and washed her hair, and dressed in fresh clothes. They were due to fly home tomorrow but she couldn't see that happening now. Even so, she put a few items of clothing into her suitcase to pass the time, cushioning the roll of canvas in a few tee-shirts. She sat leafing through an English magazine she'd brought with her but barely glanced at the advertised new fashions, hairstyles, makeup, and interior designs. Occasionally she glanced at her suitcase lost in thought. Vivien jumped, startled when a hammering at the door brought her back from daydreaming.

'Oh!' Vivien said after she'd opened the door and the banging stopped. Two men stood in the doorway. The elder and taller waved a badge in front of her eyes and although Vivien didn't take it out of his hand to read it, she knew what it was.

'Detective Inspector Berardi,' he said introducing himself, 'and this is Poliziotto Aurelio. Mrs Anderson, would you take a seat for a moment, please. There is something I must speak to you about.'

Vivien obeyed and waited. The detective was impeccably dressed. He gave a formal appearance, and his fixed expression was far from casual.

'When did you last see your husband, Mrs Anderson?'

Vivien looked from one man to the other. 'Mark? I had breakfast with him this morning, why?' When had lying become so easy, she thought.

Berardi sighed and took a seat beside her on the sofa. 'I'm sorry to be the one to tell you, Mrs Anderson. Your husband's body has been found in the River Tiber.' He waited for a response and kindly laid his hand on Vivien's.

Vivien met the Inspector's eyes, noticing they were a startlingly clear grey. She wondered what he could read in hers and waited to hear what else the detective had to say.

'I'm sorry, but I do need to ask you some questions. 'Where did you go after breakfast?'

'I'm not sure about Mark. I was going to go for a walk around Piazza Navona one last time, but I changed my mind.'

Berardi nodded with a quick curving of his lips forming a slight smile. 'So where did you go, a walk by the river perhaps?'

Idly, Vivien fingered the handle of her clutch bag, then opened it and pulled out a tissue. It seemed appropriate. She wondered how the Inspector knew she had been by the river and hoped he didn't notice the tremor in her hands or misconstrue her lack of an answer.

It interested Berardi that she hadn't asked him how her husband had died. Was she worried the information would be too upsetting or did she already know? As if she'd read his thoughts, he heard her say.

'How did Mark die? Was he in another accident?'

'Oh yes, we learned from the concierge at the reception that your husband was involved in a hit and run. He didn't report it to the police. Do you have any idea why?'

'He was only discharged from the hospital yesterday morning. Perhaps he didn't have time.'

'At the moment, we're unsure about the cause of your husband's death and must wait until after the autopsy. Drowning is the most obvious conclusion, but we're also considering his death as a possible murder.' Berardi paused to let this sink in, again waiting for a response from her. 'Your husband was badly beaten before going into the river.' The detective's words were intentionally harsh. He felt an urge to break Vivien's composure.

Poliziotto Aurelio stood waiting near the door. He shifted his position and when Berardi glanced his way, Aurelio raised his eyebrows questioningly. Berardi gave a slight nod in his direction and then turned his attention back to Vivien.

'The concierge also told us about another upsetting occurrence a few days ago. Your hotel room was ransacked. Have you any idea why your room, in particular, was targeted?'

Vivien shook her head in reply.

'Was anything stolen?'

'Not that I'm aware of, no.'

'Were they searching for something specific?'

'How would I know? Do you think it has something to do with Mark's death?'

Berardi ignored the question. 'A pair of crutches was found on the towpath underneath St Angelo's Bridge. With a broken leg it's likely your husband lost his balance and fell into the river, although it doesn't explain his severe injuries. Also, if he was using his crutches, I'm surprised they didn't fall into the river with him?'

'How would Mark have managed to get down to the river with a broken leg? Someone must have helped him?' Vivien said matter of fact.

Berardi looked at her in surprise. 'That's a good point,' Mrs Anderson. 'Was your husband a heavy drinker?'

'Yes, Mark does, did, like his whisky.' Vivien sniffed into her tissue.

'We'll need you to identify your husband's body. This is an unpleasant task but the sooner it is done the better. I have spoken to the hotel manager and have extended your stay here for another week. This room is reserved for your continual use. When we have a clearer picture of the circumstances surrounding your husband's death, and you are eliminated from our inquiries, you will be allowed to return to the UK. In the meantime, I insist you stay here in Rome. Do you have any family you wish notified?' he asked considerately.

There was Isobel, but Vivien couldn't bear the thought of the police relaying the bad news to her, so she replied that there wasn't.

Berardi went on. 'Of course, arrangements need to be made to have your husband's body returned to the UK, but it will be up to the coroner to say when this can take place. He watched Vivien dab her eyes with the tissue but couldn't see any tears. He stood to leave. There was another matter on his mind. Now perhaps was not the best time for further questioning. Even so, he felt compelled to ask. 'There's one more thing, Mrs Anderson. From a reliable source, we learned that your husband brought uncut diamonds into this country. Do you know for what purpose and where they are now?'

Vivien took a breath. 'No.'

'We believe they were used as payment for a stolen painting recently available for sale on the black market. Were you aware of your husband's involvement in this?'

'I know he was interested in several paintings which had been found in Milan. Mark read in the newspaper just after we arrived that they were coming to Rome to be authenticated and then put on display. He was excited about being able to view them while we were here. What makes you think the painting is valuable?'

Berardi frowned. 'What do you mean?'

'If it is one of the paintings from the find in Milan and stolen before being authenticated, there's no way of knowing what it is worth if anything at all.'

Berardi stared at Vivien. 'The painting in question is a genuine Caravaggio, and I didn't say it was one of the paintings found in Milan? What made you think it is?'

'I suppose I just assumed?' Vivien suddenly wished she'd kept her mouth shut.

'You seem to know a lot about the art world, Mrs Anderson.'

'Mark and I run an Art and Antique business at home, so I do know a little. Mark was the art expert, though.'

Berardi listened to Vivien weighing her up. Closed up was how he would have described her a few minutes ago, but at the mention of the stolen painting, she had suddenly found her voice. 'Please, let us accompany you to the Funeral Office now.' He stood and waited for Vivien to collect her jacket and then they both followed the policeman, Aurelio, out of the room.

After the ordeal of identifying the body of her husband, Vivien returned to the comfort of her hotel room. She'd hardly had any time to recover from that or the police visit earlier when her door was hammered on again. Vivien opened it and David Lanceley rushed in.

'My God, Viv, is it true. They're saying downstairs that Mark is dead.'

'Yes, he is. I won't be going home tomorrow. I've got to stay behind for the inquest.' Vivien had a sudden thought. 'Have the police questioned you?'

'They spoke to me briefly just now. They asked if I knew anything about a stolen Caravaggio painting and if Mark had mentioned anything about it to me.'

'What did you say?'

'Nothing, well, I told them he'd invited me to go with him to the Galleria to ask if the paintings found in Milan had arrived, but that I'd declined the invitation. Did he ever get there, by the way, the Galleria?'

Vivien shrugged. 'No idea. He never mentioned that he had to me.'

'Forget that for a moment. How about I delay my return for another week, then at least you will have some company.' Seeing how pale she was, David took her in his arms and hugged her.

'I'm all right, David.' Vivien spoke to his shoulder as she struggled out of his grip.

'You're not all right, you look ghastly. You've had a terrible shock.'

'You're very kind to offer to prolong your holiday for me but think about how it would look. The police may decide we're having a relationship. They could say it's a motive for his murder. Besides I don't want you dragged into this mess.'

'Murder, what are you talking about?'

'Detective Inspector Berardi believes Mark may have been murdered.'

'I didn't realise. I thought he'd had another accident, a fatal one this time.'

'I don't want to talk about it, David, but you do see my point don't you?'

'Yes, I suppose you're right, it would look bad. I should go and start packing then. You're sure you'll be okay.' David considered telling Vivien about the money Mark had borrowed from him. He'd never get that back. He consoled himself with the fact that he owned shares in Anderson Antiques, another lucrative investment for him. He would play a larger part in Vivien's life and maybe she would come to love him again. With this happy thought, he said. 'Keep in touch won't you, and let me know as soon as you get home.'

Vivien managed a smile and nodded reassuringly. 'I will, and would you check on Isobel if you have time?'

'I will, of course. Take care, Viv.'

CHAPTER 14

Vivien

I knew sooner or later the Detective Inspector would be back so my immediate worry was what to do with the painting now that I had it. I could take it to the Villa Borghese Galleria where it belonged. I'd have to disguise myself with a blonde wig and sunglasses and wear a reversible raincoat. Then after handing in the painting, all wrapped up in brown paper, of course, I'd nip into the ladies' toilets and become me again in a different jacket. I'd seen the same thing happen in a movie. Was it Audrey Hepburn in Charade? Maybe not, but anyway I couldn't do it.

I opened the roll of canvas and again studied the beautiful piece of art that had cost Mark his life. What held me in awe was the concentration on the face of the boy for such a simple task. His head tilted slightly, his eyes downcast looking at the knife in his hand. The left side of his face half in shadow. The collared shirt lay open exposing a pale hairless chest and the ivory fabric which draped his young arms showed pale wrists and suntanned hands. The folds in his shirt sleeves had been painted with such clarity you could almost believe your fingers could touch the softness of the cloth. Typically Caravaggio's light and shade phenomena.

The painting wasn't in great condition. It had a slight tear in one corner and a few jagged edges. I hadn't helped by bending it to make it fit in the rucksack. I placed the painting on the bed hardly able to draw my eyes away from the incredible work of art.

On the landing not far from my room I'd noticed the housekeeper with her cleaning trolley outside the door of a large built-in cupboard. I made sure to lock the door to the room before nipping out to explore. No one else was around, most likely in the foyer being questioned by the police. Luckily the cupboard was unlocked and inside I found spare rolls of toilet paper, bathroom necessities, clean towels, sheets, blankets, and pillowcases stacked on shelves. No one would miss a pillowcase so I took one. Back in my room, I slipped the painting inside the pillowcase and then placed it in my suitcase, again cushioned between my clothes. With a sudden flash of practicality, I remembered the painting had yet to be authenticated and so worth very little. I didn't care. I made up my mind there and then that I wasn't going to give it back.

As expected I didn't sleep that night. The events of the previous few days replayed themselves over and over in my mind as if on a loop. As dawn broke I began to panic. My emotions were in turmoil. The police were bound to want to search the room looking for the diamonds, and no doubt the painting too. How stupid of me to hide the painting in my suitcase. I knew they would have to obtain a search warrant first and that could take a day or two. It gave me a little more time.

So, where could I hide it? It was just a room in a modern hotel. No nooks and crannies. Two enormous prints adorned the walls, one a superb view of the symmetry of Bernini's colonnade taken from the Vatican's dome. The Cortile Della Pigna with its niche and pine cone atop the marble steps hung next to it. I contemplated sticking the canvas behind one of those, but what with, cellotape? No, it was probably the first place the Polizia would look.

I took the pillowcase containing the canvas and

hurried back to the cleaner's cupboard. I thought the blankets the most unlikely item anyone would need in the middle of June and I lifted off a pile of neatly folded blankets and placed them to one side. The painting, minus the pillowcase, I laid flat on top of the remaining ones. I replaced the first pile of blankets and hid my Caravaggio. I tidied them making sure the folded edges were straight and didn't look as though they had been disturbed. The folded blankets overhung the shelf by a few centimetres making my treasure completely invisible. For a few moments, I stood at various positions within the cupboard until I was satisfied. It isn't just Bernini that likes symmetry.

I spent the next few days waiting for the police to return, too frightened to leave my room lest they should come and ransack it while I wasn't there. Not that there was anything to find now but anxiety overrode my senses. I used room service for my meals and no one questioned it. Considering my recent bereavement, everyone accepted it as normal. I didn't even have to feign illness. By the middle of the third day, I'd finished reading a novel and all the magazines and hotel information leaflets. The English speaking television channels on offer to view I found boring. The Italian and foreign-speaking channels I couldn't understand. I had to get out of my room.

I decided to take lunch on the terrace overlooking a busy piazza. The warmth and fresh air after being cooped up like a battery hen was a joy. The bruises on my face and neck had almost disappeared so I pushed my hair behind my ears. The roof terrace was almost empty and I waited for my lunch to be served enjoying the tranquillity. Ten minutes later Helena came over carrying two coffees and my peace was disturbed. She placed one in front of me and sat down on a chair opposite. She looked dreadful, and I could tell she had been crying.

'How are you, Vivien, I thought you might like a latte.' Helena placed her hand on my arm.

I looked down unable to meet her hazel eyes. She was upset about something and more so than I if it was because of Mark's death. I met her distress with a slight smile. 'Thanks, I'm okay, you look done in though.' I said.

Helena burst into tears. 'My father had a heart attack and passed away a few days ago, and now they've arrested Antonio for Mark's murder. It's ridiculous. Antonio wouldn't kill anyone least of all Mark. He had a great deal of respect for your husband's knowledge in the art world.'

I thought about how Mark had been beaten. Antonio may not have been the one to deliver the blows but he had most definitely instigated it. Nevertheless, I felt a degree of sadness seeing her so upset. 'I'm so sorry to hear about your father. Should you still be at work? I'm sure you would prefer to be at home with your family.'

'I'm taking some time off after today.' Helena replied. She wiped tears away from her eyes and face.

'Are you sure they've arrested Antonio for murder?' I tried to sound as if I cared and spoke as gently as I could muster. I wasn't really surprised but attempted to give the impression I was.

'Well, not arrested. The Polizia picked Antonio up. They've taken him to be questioned. He's their prime suspect.'

'I'm not so sure he is. Berardi gave me quite a grilling too, and they always suspect the spouse first, don't they? It must be very worrying for you, Helena. If there's anything I can do to help, please let me know.' I smiled and took a sip of my latte. Helena looked at me fixedly.

It made me feel uncomfortable and I readied myself for what she was about to say.

'Antonio said you were seen on St Angelo's bridge the day Mark died.'

I was taken aback by Helena's sudden directness. 'What is he implying?' I asked a tad annoyed.

'He thinks you might have seen something that could help the police with their investigation.' Helena leaned forward across the table towards me, almost pleading. 'If you know anything, Vivien, please tell the police to help, Antonio.'

'I was on the bridge. I had to walk across it to get back to the hotel after I had been out for the day. It's the only way I know. Why, is there a quicker way?' I couldn't bring myself to tell her that Antonio's bully boys had just finished beating up Mark and had left him badly injured on the towpath. For all I knew, she was as much involved in the art theft scam as her brother, an accomplice in his criminal activity. 'If Antonio is innocent then he has nothing to worry about, does he?' I stood as I spoke. I couldn't wait to escape back to the safety of my room.

My room wasn't safe. My worst fear was taking place and I almost cried out when I saw Poliziotto Aurelio and three other policemen in my room going through our belongings. Aurelio waved a search warrant in front of my eyes. With my heart pounding and my fingers crossed I prayed they wouldn't decide to search the cleaner's cupboard down the corridor. I waited by the door for them to finish, not letting myself consider the consequences should the painting be found? Finally, the policemen emerged one by one. Only Aurelio remained and he beckoned me inside.

'Thank you, Mrs Anderson; I'm sorry for the disruption.' He took a cigarette out of a half-empty packet and flicked open his lighter.

'No smoking if you don't mind,' I told him sharply pointing to a no-smoking sign, then the offending items and the door.

Aurelio paused with his cigarette halfway to his lips and then sighed. He complied grudgingly and then followed his colleagues.

The people working in the hotel have been kind to me but after a day or two, their consolatory manner got on my nerves. More tourists arrived and I soon realised they'd been informed of my bereavement. I'd begun to use the hotel restaurant again for my meals but whenever I entered I sensed a hush. An elderly gentleman tried to befriend me and asked if he could join me for dinner. When I tactfully explained I would prefer to dine alone he became affronted and implied I should be grateful for the attention. I wasn't grateful.

Helena looks ill with worry. It seems a witness, presumably someone from our tour party, reported that they saw Mark and Antonio together on our visit to the Trevi Fountain. I'm spending most of my time trying to avoid her.

I'd been putting off ringing Isobel for as long as could when I remembered I'd asked David to go and see her. I knew she would never forgive me if I left it to David to break the news about her father's death. I finally plucked up the courage but the conversation with my daughter has left me feeling tense.

I couldn't bring myself to tell her that her father may have been murdered, or go into the details of his death over the telephone. The distance between us didn't help and I don't just mean the geographical miles. So I did what I thought best and told her Mark had gone for a walk and ended up on the towpath underneath St. Angelo's bridge. He'd been drinking and so the police believe he became disorientated and toppled over into the river. I didn't bother to mention his previous road accident knowing it would result in questions I wouldn't be able to answer. I listened dry-eyed to Isobel's sobs.

'Where were you when it happened, Mum,' she questioned, her tone accusing.

'I was in the hotel.'

'How come he went for a walk on his own? Was he meeting someone?' Isobel blew her nose.

I wasn't surprised by the question. Isobel knew if her father hadn't taken me with him then he probably had a prearranged assignation. 'I don't know, Isobel. The Police came to see me around nine p.m. They'd had an anonymous telephone call earlier that evening to tell them a body was floating in the River Tiber. It turned out to be your father.' I hesitated. 'I'm so sorry to be the bearer of bad news, dear.'

'A body, he's just a body to you now? That's my father you're talking about.'

I felt as though my face had been slapped and I took a breath to compose myself. 'I'll be home as soon as I can, hopefully by the end of the week.' I managed to say.

'You hated him, didn't you? I bet you're glad he's dead.' Isobel shouted at me down the line.

Relieved was the word I would have chosen but I said nothing. I let her words hang in the air, probably somewhere over France.

'Sorry, if that upset you.' Isobel snapped.

'I can hear in your voice that you're angry with me,' I replied quietly. 'You're upset and I understand. I'll telephone you again in a couple of days to let you know what's happening, and the date when I'll be home. Goodbye Isobel.' I didn't wait for her reply. Her words had stung. It seemed my daughter had venom in her veins just like her father.

CHAPTER 15

The Capo Della Polizia, *The Chief of Police*, was hounding Berardi for results and Berardi sat at his desk looking at the information he and his team had gathered. It wasn't often he became despondent but the death of Mark Anderson had him baffled. The lack of concrete evidence against their main suspect, Antonio Cortez, meant that soon, to detain him any longer wouldn't be an option. He had been over all the facts so many times he almost knew the details off by heart. Aurelio, his sergeant, had also scrutinised every detail but his efforts had turned out to be fruitless too.

Then, of course, Berardi had the problem of the stolen painting. Art theft wasn't part of his department's criteria as far as Berardi was concerned, or it hadn't been until recently. Rumoured news of an alleged Caravaggio available on the black market had set the slow-moving wheels of the cold case inquiry into a spin. Berardi didn't have much faith in the Polizia Locale in charge of the investigation in Milan and the surrounding area. He'd considered sending Aurelio to shake things up a bit and then dismissed it. He needed him here in Rome, but someone else had to go and fast. He was annoyed he hadn't arranged to send a member of his team sooner. For now, it gave him something positive to do and he lifted the telephone receiver to arrange the secondment.

After making the call Berardi picked up all the statements again and flicked through them one by one. Cortez had been held in custody now for the permitted time. Berardi knew it was futile to request an extension without any new evidence concerning the case. They had found several paintings in his apartment, which at first glance appeared to be genuine and had caused a great deal of speculation. An art authenticator's closer inspection proved them all to be fakes. Cortez had denied being on the towpath the day of Mr Anderson's death and had an alibi to confirm it. Berardi's sensitive gut told him Cortez was involved both in Mr Anderson's death and the stolen painting. It was a pity he hadn't the means to prove it.

Then there was Helena Cortez, Antonio's younger sister. From several conversations with guests staying at the Hotel, Berardi heard there appeared to have been a romantic connection between her and Mark Anderson. Did Helena's involvement with Mark, a much older man, have another agenda? Had Antonio encouraged the friendship for reasons of his own? Berardi made a note to interview her again.

The next was David Lanceley, who had now left Italy on his scheduled flight home. Later, after Berardi had spoken to guests at the hotel, he'd learned that Lanceley and Vivien Anderson had had a close relationship before he began studying theology. He'd gone on to serve as vicar at an Anglican church for a few years in the village where Vivien Anderson now lived. Lanceley then decided to leave the church and Berardi pondered what the reason could have been. Also, how did the guests, who supposedly had never met David or Vivien before, know these personal details? Was it just gossip, something to speculate about in-between tours? Or had the couple rekindled their romance? If that was true it gave Lanceley, and Vivien, a motive for Mark Anderson's murder? No longer a man of God, had Lanceley thrown away his good conscious as well as his cassock?

Finally, there was Vivien, an enigma to him. Berardi

leaned back in his chair, holding her statement. He sensed an underlying passion beneath her cool almost icy disposition. He'd noticed the bruises the first time he met her, although at the time he was so absorbed in his job he hadn't given it much thought. Later he wished he'd asked her how she had come by them. Had she fallen? Maybe her husband had caused them. Berardi thought again of David Lanceley and took into account an added reason for a motive.

Berardi found it difficult to believe what was staring him in the face. Mark Anderson's death was an accident. His injuries, the coroner had confirmed, could have been caused by the fall into the river and the subsequent bashing against the bridge's ramparts. He had been drinking and his toxicology report showed that there was enough alcohol in his system to render him almost comatose. Not improbable then, so fallen in, not pushed. Berardi's gut told him otherwise.

Cortez would have to be released and there was no reason to delay Mrs Anderson's return home to the UK any longer. He had other cases needing his attention. Berardi put all the statements back into Mark Anderson's file but kept it in front of him on his desk. He would get to the bottom of this eventually, he usually did. Berardi picked up the telephone again, and then replaced it when Aurelio entered the room.

'Find anything?' Berardi asked him.

Aurelio sat down at his desk in the corner of the room and swung his chair around to face his boss. 'Nothing of interest; we had the room to ourselves for a while too, and we were thorough, but.....' Aurelio shook his head, opened his hands' palms upwards and shrugged.

'Did you see Mrs Anderson and get a chance to speak to her again?' Berardi slipped Vivien's statement out of the folder and scanned through it again.

'She came back just as we'd finished. In a foul mood

by the looks of it too so I didn't hang around.' Aurelio looked at his watch. 'Cortez's time is up, are we going for an extension?'

'No. Let him go, but arrange to have an eye kept on him, day and night for the next few days at least.'

'What about Mrs Anderson?'

'What about her?'

'Are we bringing her in for questioning?'

'Do you think she's involved?'

'She was agitated when she saw us searching her room, but she's not the type to commit murder, is she?'

'Looks can be deceiving, Aurelio, you should have learned that by now. I'll go and have another word with her later. Hopefully, now that she's had a few days to come to terms with her husband's death, she may have remembered something useful.'

'Do you want me to come with you?' Aurelio asked half-heartedly. His stomach rumbled loudly so he added as an apology, 'I had to work through my lunch hour.'

Berardi shook his head. 'No, get something to eat. I'll see you back here in a couple of hours.' Berardi was about to put on his jacket when his desk phone rang.

'Hello, Berardi here.'

'Jack Tyler, Pietro. Have you got time for a chat?'

CHAPTER 16

Vivien

Detective Inspector Berardi came to tell me I can go home. He's offered to make the arrangements for Mark's remains to be transported to the aeroplane on the day of my flight. I'm grateful but I consider it's the least he can do under the circumstances. I know he's still suspicious of me. He made it obvious by going over my statement again, asking me questions he'd already asked what seems like a hundred times. My answers are still the same.

During the question and answer debacle, Berardi let it drop into the conversation that Antonio has been released. He went on to explain that as no firm evidence had come to light to incriminate Antonio in Mark's death, they couldn't hold him in custody any longer. I think he expected a reaction from me and although I was dismayed by the news I did a good job of hiding it. The coroner's verdict earlier that day had stated that in his opinion, Mark Anderson had been drinking became dizzy and fell into the river, and this had clinched Antonio's release.

My flight has been arranged for tomorrow. I'm so anxious I just want to be gone now. I've tried ringing Jack but he's either ignoring my calls or has his mobile switched off. I think just hearing his voice would help. I'm so afraid and my panic levels are high. Every time I hear a noise in the hall outside, or if there's a knock on my door, I'm ready to dive for cover, believing Antonio or his two henchmen have come for me. If only I hadn't taken the painting from Jack? If only he was here to keep me safe. Tears have begun to come and go unheeded these days and it doesn't help knowing I brought this terror on myself.

I retrieved the painting, Boy Peeling Fruit, from the cleaner's cupboard without any mishap and it's safely packed away in one of the new suitcases I've had to buy to replace the ones destroyed in the ransacking of our hotel room. Mark's case I packed a few days ago and it's stood by the door ready to go.

A taxi picked me up at the hotel early this morning and I've just arrived at the airport. I paid the taxi driver and while he unloaded the luggage I looked around me, wondering if Antonio would dare to show his face and try to hinder my departure. I haven't seen Helena for a few days now. I know she'll be relieved Antonio is no longer under suspicion.

The driver has brought me a luggage trolley and put the two cases on it. He bid me *arrivederci* and climbed back in his cab. I pushed the trolley through the automatic opening doors leading into Leonardo da Vinci Airport di Roma and stood for a moment wondering what to do next. I made for the departure lounge and saw Jack as soon as I entered. He was standing beside a kiosk selling newspapers and cigarettes attempting to be inconspicuous. The description 'tall dark and handsome,' fitted perfectly. He turned heads and not only mine. My stomach did a funny flip as it always did when he was near. How anyone could miss seeing him was a mystery to me. He was looking the other way but I sensed that he'd seen me. Shame washed over me. He'd trusted me, made love to me, and I'd stolen from him. No matter he had done the same when he stole the key Caplan gave me.

I couldn't face him or speak to him so I began to walk in the other direction. I made for the computer screens showing departure flights and the check-in desk I needed for my Manchester flight. I knew I had blown it with Jack and it saddened me.

I saw another face that I wanted to avoid, and I brushed Jack from my mind. My heart sank because I knew this man wouldn't be easy to get rid of. I'd only walked a few metres when I heard his voice calling my name. I had no choice but to turn and watch Detective Inspector Berardi walk towards me.

Berardi didn't smile as he drew nearer. If he had it wouldn't have reached his eyes. It never did. He maintained his calm persona and sombre expression as he said. 'Mrs Anderson, I thought it was you.' He smiled then, but his grey eyes were as ever cold and calculating. 'May I have a word?'

'Hello again,' I replied tersely and began to walk on again with Berardi at my heels.

'I thought, as you're returning home alone, you may need help with your suitcases. Perhaps you'll allow me to assist you.' His eyes rested on the two cases side by side on the trolley.

'Thank you, I'm fine.' I clung on to my rucksack as if my life depended on its nearness. Berardi was like a limpet I couldn't shake off.

'The checking in desk you need is this way,' he said, taking my elbow.

Knowing it was useless to resist, I allowed myself to be escorted through the throng of other passengers who were heading the other way towards security desks. I checked in my luggage and together, Berardi and I watched the cases shudder along the conveyor belt out of sight. The policeman remained stuck beside me on the way to security and his presence began to unnerve me. I took my place behind a queue of other travellers and had my passport and boarding card ready for inspection. Suddenly the policeman took my elbow again and pulled me to one side.

'Mrs Anderson, are you not curious about your husband at all? You don't seem concerned to know whether his coffin has been safely placed into the cargo hold on the aeroplane.'

I looked at him with as much indignation as I could muster. 'You told me you would arrange everything. I trusted that you had.' I saw his lips move but he spoke so softly I couldn't hear the words. I moved away to try and regain my place in the queue but Berardi hadn't finished. He held up a small cylinder gold case, took off the lid and wound up the bright pink lipstick held inside.

'Is this yours? It's very like the colour you wear.' He held it up against my face.

I reached inside my bag conscious my hands were trembling and pulled out the compulsory plastic bag to pass through security. It contained my inhaler and a lipstick, Estee Lauder's Candy Shimmer. 'No Inspector, mine is here. Why would you think it was mine?' I retrieved it from the bag for him to see.' Berardi's surprised face cheered me. I wanted to laugh and shout, see I didn't do it.

'It was found by one of our divers in the River Tiber, near where we think your husband fell in.'

'Do you still believe my husband was murdered then, and that a woman was involved? The coroner's verdict was accidental death by downing, wasn't it? Surely the case is now closed.'

Berardi frowned at me disgruntled. He put the offending lipstick back into his pocket and finally he let me go.

CHAPTER 17

Jack stood out of view observing Vivien and his friend Pietro Berardi, and if he hadn't known better he might have believed they were a couple. The way the detective stood just that little bit too close, bending slightly and speaking into her ear. She was looking up at him with wide innocent eyes listening. No one would guess that the only thing she had on her mind was escaping that man. No one would guess that the only thing he had on his mind was a valuable painting and murder.

Jack had seen Vivien as she stepped out of the taxi on her arrival at the airport. She didn't see him. He had made sure of that. If he hadn't already met her and known about her bereavement, he would still have guessed something was troubling her. The way her shoulders hitched a little too high and the slightly hunched look as if she was about to fold in on herself. She hadn't bothered with makeup and devoid of it her face was pale and colourless. Her long dark hair hung loose even though there was no need to hide bruises now. To him, Vivien looked as stunning as ever and he noticed that he wasn't the only man showing an interest. Vivien's appeal was real and natural, a quality most men found irresistible. Her usual attire of shift dress, cardigan or jacket and high heels, she'd replaced with cream coloured chinos, a white fitted shirt and a cropped denim jacket, together with comfortable looking loafers. An outfit one wouldn't expect to be worn by someone who was supposed to be in mourning.

Jack knew that his interest in her had to be entirely professional from now on. He had made the mistake of letting his heart, and another important part of his body, rule his head, but he wouldn't let that happen again. As a Customs and Excise investigator who specialised in art crime, he needed to remain focused. As he watched Vivien and Berardi in deep discussion, he questioned Inspector's Berardi's decision to let Vivien leave the country.

Vivien took her seat on the aeroplane and pushed her rucksack under the seat in front of her and then fastened the safety belt ready for take-off. She didn't know if it was the prospect of flying alone or the effects of the last few days finally catching up with her but suddenly she felt very tired. She closed her eyes and thought about what she'd done. She became aware of someone closing the overhead locker above her and felt whoever it was, take the vacant seat beside her. For a moment she imagined it was Mark and the stuff of nightmares filled her mind. Vivien glanced in the person's direction but the man's face was turned away but only for a moment. She watched Jack's long fingers deftly clip in his safety belt and recognised the Paco Rabanne aftershave. She enjoyed the waft of freshly showered skin as it drifted towards her and suddenly she was there in his arms again, remembering their time in bed together and how breathtakingly wonderful it was.

The aircraft moved along the runway and a steady hum vibrated through the seat. Vivien thought about Caravaggio, his life and the wrong choices he'd made. She thought about her own recent choices and wondered what consequences were in store for her. She thought about the Caravaggio painting Mark had so desperately wanted to own, flat in her suitcase among her underwear. She thought how ironic it was that right now Mark was in touching distance of it.

Jack ordered a whisky and sat reading a book, ignoring Vivien. She stared out of the small oval window at pillows of white clouds, dented and squashed into irregular shapes. At last, she could stand it no longer.

'So, you're returning to Manchester today too, what a coincidence?'

Jack turned his head to look at her with an unblinking stare and then turned away again. He spoke to the passenger sitting in the aisle seat next to him who immediately rose to let him pass. Jack was gone for about five minutes and when he returned he continued to read his book.

'I'm sorry, okay? I took the painting to get back at you for stealing the key from me.'

Jack closed his book and adjusted his seat, then closed his eyes and appeared to doze.

'Don't speak to me then,' Vivien said crossly. 'It's your loss.' To Vivien's dismay, Jack smirked. Was it in response to her words or something he'd read earlier? Vivien knew why Jack was acting this way and she couldn't blame him. A few days ago she'd hoped for a future with him, but because of her stupidity, and coveting a worthless painting, all that had faded into the prospect of gloom.

CHAPTER 18

The aircraft landed and manoeuvred its way towards the arrival door where the passengers could alight. Vivien was asked to wait until everyone else had left the aircraft before being accompanied off the aeroplane. Jack Tyler had disappeared into the crowd without a backward glance.

A tall man in his late fifties approached her on the tarmac. 'Mrs Anderson, Hello. My name is Eric Hennessey.' The funeral director was dressed for work in a black suit and tie. He shook Vivien's hand and offered his condolences, and then suggested she leave the details of transporting the coffin back to the funeral parlour to him. Vivien was grateful to have the burden lifted from her shoulders and thanked him, shaking his hand vigorously. Mr Hennessey assured her he would call to see her the next day to finalise the arrangements for her husband's burial.

The other passengers including, Jack, had already collected their suitcases and Vivien and Mark's luggage appeared on the conveyor belt looking lost and alone. Just how she felt, thought Vivien, as she made her way through customs and looked around for a familiar face.

Instantly, David appeared by her side as if by magic, every feature on his face showed joy. 'Viv, at last, I wondered where you'd got to.' He kissed her lightly on the cheek.

'Is Isobel with you?' Vivien asked hopefully.

'No. I called to pick her up but she decided to wait at

home. You know Isobel.' David put his arm around Vivien's shoulders. 'Come on let's get you into the car.'

On the way home, David tried his best to make conversation. Vivien was having none of it. She was determined to avoid answering questions so feigned tiredness and closed her eyes. Eventually, David got the message. As soon as the car pulled up outside Lilac House, Isobel was at the door. She stood with her arms wrapped around her waist as though for protection, the look on her face unwelcoming. David began to unload the suitcases, sensibly keeping his distance.

Isobel forced a smile and stepped back to let Vivien through the door. 'How was your flight?' she asked dutifully.

'The flight was fine, thanks.' Vivien took a long look at her daughter. 'Are you okay?'

'What do you think?' Isobel stared back at her mother.

'Yes, I'm sorry. It's been a terrible shock for you.'

'Do you want tea or something?' Isobel said over her shoulder as she flounced into the kitchen.

'Tea will be lovely.' Vivien followed her. Her daughter wore her grief like a garment, and the biblical expression sackcloth and ashes came to Vivien's mind. She was glad to notice her daughter looked healthy and well-fed. At least her appetite hadn't been affected by her father's demise, she thought. Isobel favoured Mark's colouring and her golden skin tone and blonde hair shone with health. Although sad, as always her bright blue eyes had an impish look, as if she was just about to do something naughty. Mark had had the same expression and it pained Vivien to look at Isobel and see her father. She recalled Berardi's remark about her seemingly lack of sorrow and wondered if that bothered, Isobel too?

Vivien left Isobel to make the tea and walked into the

sitting room. David came in and stood at the door.

'I've put the cases in the hall for now. I'll take yours upstairs before I go. I don't like to mention it but what do you want me to do with Mark's case.' He spoke in an undertone, almost reverently, and she was reminded of his previous occupation.

'Leave them both in the hall, for now, thanks. You don't have to walk on eggshells with me, David.' Vivien said, also lowering her voice. 'You might need to with Isobel though.'

'Where is she?' David asked.

'In the kitchen making tea,' Vivien smiled. 'I know you'd prefer a beer. Go through, there's sure to be one in the fridge.' After a few moments, Vivien heard David and Isobel's voices. Soft mumbling and then Isobel laughed. They weren't discussing Mark's death then? Suddenly her daughter's voice could be heard loud and clear.

'Well, I'm going whether Mum likes it or not.'

Vivien stood and went to join them. David's glass of beer was poured and he was in the process of pouring tea into two mugs. Isobel stood at the worktop taking cling film off a plate of sandwiches.

'What's going on?' Vivien asked, looking from one to the other.

'Ah Vivien, Come on, sit down and have this.' David walked back into the sitting room with the tea. Isobel brushed past her carrying the sandwiches and almost flung them onto the coffee table.

'I heard you say you're going somewhere, Isobel, and you don't care whether I like it or not? Will one of you explain please?'

'Isobel wants to see where her father died. She's booked herself a flight to Rome. I've been trying to talk her out of it, that's why I never mentioned it before. It's understandable why she wants to go.' David looked at

Vivien ruefully.

'I see.' Vivien waited for her daughter to elaborate. Isobel took a sandwich and started munching.

Vivien moved the place of sandwiches out of her daughter's reach and waited until she'd finished eating before saying. 'When are you going?'

'In three days, and I'll be staying in the same hotel as you and Dad.'

'If going will help you come to terms with your father's death then I'm fine with it.' Vivien picked up a sandwich and after a few mouthfuls realised how hungry she was. She hadn't fancied eating anything on the aeroplane, not with Jack's disapproving presence next to her. 'These are very good,' she praised,' reaching for another. If Isobel was expecting her to create a scene, then she was in for a disappointment. Experience had taught Vivien that this was the best way to handle her daughter, and besides, she was tired of all the bickering. On her flight home, she'd decided that she was going to start to take control of her own life, and allow Isobel to do the same. After all, her daughter wasn't a child to be mollycoddled any longer. Vivien hadn't wanted Isobel to grow up thinking everything in life was easy, and people's feelings didn't matter. Or, to get what you wanted all you had to do was kick up a fuss, but Mark had given in to Isobel's every whim. Vivien knew deep down that her daughter's attitude towards her was due to Mark's influence, so she'd made allowances for Isobel's continual disrespect. Vivien was comforted with the thought that in her effort to change, to become stronger and self-reliant, maybe Isobel would come to like her, even love her again, as she once did.

'I thought you'd object,' Isobel said.

'Not at all, but I am surprised you didn't decide to wait until after your father's funeral before heading off.' Vivien replied quietly.

'I thought Dad's funeral would take place before I go?' Isobel looked horrified.

'I doubt it. Mr Hennessey, the undertaker, met me at the airport when I arrived. He's coming tomorrow to discuss the arrangements.'

'What shall I do, then?' Isobel looked at David for help.

'I'm sure you could change your booking for a later week. It may be more awkward with your flight but there's no harm in trying. Do you want me to see what I can do?'

Isobel rushed off upstairs to get the relevant paperwork and after handing the responsibility over to David to sort it out, she sat back down next to her mother. David disappeared into the kitchen and they could hear him tapping numbers into his iPad.

'Mum, if it makes you feel any better, I'm not going alone. Grace Farrell has offered to come with me. She's been very supportive. I don't know what I'd have done without her these last few days. As soon as she heard about Dad's death she came to see me. Her parents died in a car crash when she was a teenager, did you know?'

'Yes, Amelia mentioned it briefly a few months ago. It was a terrible time for them both.'

David called from the kitchen.' The hotel is all sorted. I'm going to see what I can do about the flights now.'

A thought crossed Vivien's mind and she wondered whether David still harboured romantic thoughts for Amelia and regretted losing her to Peter. He had never gone into details about their brief affair, and Vivien hadn't pried. Isobel's voice brought her back to the problem at hand.

'Grace understands exactly how frustrated I feel. Not knowing what happened, needing answers to questions that are unbearable to ask. It was Grace who suggested we go and she helped me book our hotel room and flights.

'That was very thoughtful of her,' Vivien agreed.

'We're staying for five days. Having a holiday of sorts, you know, doing a bit of sightseeing. I'm looking forward to it in a funny sort of way. So, you don't mind me going, Mum.'

'As long as you promise to ring me or text when you arrive, to let me know you're safe.' Vivien laid her hand on her daughter's arm reassuringly.

'Of course, I will.' For the first time since Vivien's arrival home, Isobel had lost her tense expression.

'There is one thing I think you ought to know before you go.' Vivien said as David came back into the room.

'All fixed. Here are your new dates and flight times. You'd best let Grace know as soon as possible, just in case she makes other arrangements.' David sat and finished off the last few remaining sandwiches.

'What were you about to say, Mum?' Isobel asked.

'The Italian Coroner has recorded Accidental Death by Drowning as the reason for Mark's death. So you'll both be relieved to know he wasn't murdered as suspected after all.' Vivien looked from one to the other waiting for their response.

'Murdered? What are you talking about?' Isobel's face paled.

Too late Vivien realised she had put her foot in it. On the telephone she hadn't told Isobel all the details surrounding her father's death and now when it didn't matter, she was going to have to go over it all again. 'I didn't want to worry you but the police were suspicious at first.' She looked at David for support.

'I left for the airport the day after your father's death. When the police questioned me I had the impression they suspected foul play.'

'But why did they suspect foul play? Is there's something else you're not telling me?'

Vivien sighed, and then biting the bullet, she said, 'I know for a fact your father was interested in acquiring a painting, allegedly by Caravaggio. What I didn't know until later was that the painting he was after had been stolen. Also, he'd been seen with a known villain and so the police suspected your father may have been involved in the theft. In 2012 several paintings and sketches were discovered at Castello Sforzesco in Milan. They were to be displayed to the public in Rome while we were there. Your father was very excited about it. Do you remember David?'

'Yes, I remember thinking it was an art scam.'

'Your father was contacted just before the start of our holiday and led to believe that a painting, a genuine Caravaggio, was available for him on the black market.'

'So you knew about this, David?' Isobel stood and towered over them both, bright red spots flushed her cheeks. 'Surely Dad wasn't taken in by it?'

'It's possible; you know how obsessed he was with Caravaggio.'

'That was a pipe dream, Mum, and anyway, Dad didn't have that kind of money, did he?'

'I can't answer that,' Vivien stated.

Isobel shook her head. 'When they made these accusations did you at least try to defend him? Or did you just roll over and agree with everything "for peace sake" like you always do?'

'Please don't talk to your mother like that, Isobel. It isn't fair. You're not the only one grieving you know.'

'You think?' Isobel snapped, and then stormed off up to her room.

'Shall I go and talk to her,' David asked.

'No, leave her, let's give her some space. I'm so tired David, I think I'll have a lie-down. Would you mind carrying the cases upstairs for me before you go, please?'

With David gone and Isobel still sulking, Vivien took

a shower then climbed into bed. At that moment she didn't care if she never woke up.

CHAPTER 19

A week after the funeral, Vivien began going through cupboards and sideboards in the house. She found paperwork and receipts from years ago, and after a quick look through, she saw they were to do with their house purchase and had nothing to do with the business. She put them to one side on the coffee table promising to look at them later. Everything to do with Anderson Antiques, she placed in a separate pile. In one of the drawers in a sideboard, she found Mark's will and her own. They'd been drawn up soon after their marriage and as far as she was aware, Mark had never changed his, and neither had she. Bank statements, and shares in various companies she was unaware Mark had, she found filed in a concertina type file in the sideboard cupboard. She placed them in an A4 envelope and wrote their solicitors' address on the front ready to post. The next few days she spent sorting Mark's clothes, packing them all into refuse sacks ready to take to a charity shop. There was no sentiment or sorrow in the task as she folded them. No memories of happy days spent together when he'd worn a certain hat or shirt. To Vivien, everything in the house belonging to Mark was refuse, waiting to be got rid of.

Next, Vivien set about cleaning their bedroom and she attacked his wardrobe and tallboy as though even the dust had been contaminated by him. Mark's items, including watches and cuff links, she packed into a box destined for the loft. Out of sight and out of mind. Her only concessions to this purge were photographs and these she put in Isobel's bedroom. The rest of the house she cleaned like a woman demented. The house belonged to her now to do with as she wanted, she reminded herself. She would redo the masculine décor. Replace the black leather sofas, dark mahogany furniture and black-framed art. Her house would reflect her taste from now on, and knowing this gave Vivien purpose and something to look forward to.

Back home and in her normal surroundings again, with Isobel in Rome with Grace, reality had hit Vivien hard. She went over her actions on that fateful day wondering what on earth had possessed her. In the back of her mind, Vivien knew that all her recent industriousness was her way of stalling her foremost worry. After unpacking her suitcase she'd hidden the painting she taken from Jack's hotel room on top of her wardrobe. It couldn't stay there, though. On a continuous loop she kept asking herself, what should she do with the painting now that she had it? She couldn't hang it anywhere, couldn't let anyone set eyes on its exquisite beauty, as much as she would have liked to. Although the painting was almost undeniably a fake, who she wondered could copy a Caravaggio with the same style and clarity of colour.

Vivien sensed a headache coming on and two paracetamol and thirty minutes later she was in her car and on her way to see David. She toyed with the idea of confiding in him and then dismissed it. Although David was no longer a vicar, he still maintained very high moral standards. He was always going on about the principle of something, and stealing was a definite no-go area for him.

Relieved to see David's Jaguar parked on the driveway, Vivien locked her car and rushed to the house, eager to see him. She didn't bother to ring the front doorbell. Vivien knew from experience that David always left his back door unlocked. It was a habit left over from his previous life, an open invitation for visiting church members.

Vivien let herself in and walked straight into David's small minimalistic kitchen, spotless except for a pile of unwashed dishes in the sink. Vivien could hear David speaking and she followed the sound of his voice. When she reached the sitting-room door she saw he was on the telephone. In case it was a private matter and not wanting to intrude she waited on the other side of the door. It was impossible not to overhear his one-sided conversation and after a few minutes, she knew David was talking to Isobel. The urge to rush in and ask to speak to her daughter was strong, but Vivien decided against it. Isobel had been in Rome for two days now, and after a short text to say she had arrived safe, Vivien hadn't heard from her since. It hurt that her daughter found time to telephone David but not her mother. She listened and the more she heard, the more wounded she became.

'If that's what you want, Isobel, but it puts me in a very awkward position.' David was saying.

...

'No, I won't tell her.'

...

Okay, yes, I said. I promise I won't tell her. Have you telephoned her yet, she is bound to be worried and waiting to hear from you.'

...

'Well, I hope all goes well. Try not to get too upset. Is Grace going with you?'

...

'All right then, and don't forget to telephone your mother, Isobel.'

...

155

'Goodbye.'

...

Vivien waited until David had replaced the receiver and then walked in. 'Well, it seems as though I timed my visit just right. I apologise for eavesdropping, David, but if you don't want people to walk in, you should lock your door.'

'Vivien, I'm glad to see you,' David hugged her and led her to the sofa.

'So, you promise you won't tell me what?' she asked, challenging him.

'It isn't anything for you to worry yourself about,' David replied, ignoring her question.

'What doesn't Isobel want you to tell me, and who is she meeting?' Vivien persisted.

'You probably heard me promise I wouldn't say.'

'Don't give me any of your waffle; I'm not in the mood. I don't give a fig for your promise to Isobel. She's my daughter and I have a right to know. Where exactly does your loyalty lay?'

'Would you like a drink, I'm having one.' David stood and walked out of the room.

Exasperated Vivien followed. 'Please tell me what's going on.'

'I will, in a minute. Let's be civilised about it though. I don't want an argument.'

Vivien returned to the sitting room and waited. 'Well,' she asked once he'd sat down again and taken a sip of coffee.

'Isobel has met Helena.'

'What's the problem with me knowing that? Come on David, what else?'

'Before I say anymore, I want you to know that I only agreed to comply with Isobel's secrecy because I thought if you knew what she intended, well, you wouldn't be happy about it, that's all. I didn't want to upset you.'

'For goodness sake tell me before I throttle you.'

'Helena introduced Isobel and Grace to Antonio, and yesterday they spent some time with him.' Vivien's hands clenched as she waited for him to continue.

'It seems as soon as he knew, via Helena, that your daughter, Isobel, was in Rome, he searched her out to offer his condolences. I met Antonio once, briefly. He's a good deal older than the girls so they will be safe with him. Good for them to have someone who knows the best places to visit while travelling around sightseeing. Unsurprisingly, Isobel is smitten with him. He's very good looking, isn't he? It seems the two of them hit it off straight away. Antonio is going to take her to where he said he believes Mark fell into the river. Isobel told me she is going to put some flowers for her father on top of the bridge parapet. She got very emotional when telling me this on the telephone.'

When Vivien could, at last, bring herself to respond, all that came out of her mouth was, 'Oh!' Her throat had constricted her mouth suddenly dry. She reached for her coffee and took a sip. It scalded her lips. All sorts of "what ifs" darted her mind. What if Antonio tells Isobel about the diamonds, what they were for and her mother's involvement? What if he kidnaps Isobel and holds her to ransom? What if her daughter falls in love with him? Vivien's hands were clammy and her legs weak as she stood. 'You said something about a meeting. You asked if Grace was going to go with her.' Vivien guessed who the meeting was with before David said the name, but needed it confirming.

'Isobel has an appointment to see Detective Inspector Berardi tomorrow. Don't look so aghast, Viv. Look at it from her point of view. Surely you can understand she wants to know all the details of what happened to her father.'

'Clearly, she doesn't believe what I tell her, you forgot

to add that.' Vivien picked up her handbag and made to leave. She felt betrayed and didn't want to talk to David anymore.

'Don't go, Viv, not like this. Stay and finish your coffee at least.'

Vivien wouldn't stay. She sat outside David's house in her car for a few minutes gulping back tears. When David appeared at the door and called her name, saying he was sorry, and please come back in, she started the engine and drove off.

CHAPTER 20

Grace had been looking forward to visiting Rome with her friend, even though it wasn't a holiday as such. Looking at Isobel today, no one would guess that the reason for her visit was to mourn the recent loss of her father and pay vigil to the place where he had lost his life. Admittedly, on their first day they had stood on the towpath underneath St. Angelo's bridge and let their tears flow, Grace's in sympathy for her friend's loss. But now the tears had dried and the purpose of their visit seemingly forgotten by Isobel.

Of course, it was all down to Helena's brother, Antonio, who Isobel had fallen head over heels in love with at first sight. Grace didn't believe in love at first sight and thought the whole scenario too good to be true. Perhaps she would have felt different if Jake was with her. Maybe then she wouldn't feel so lonely and homesick.

Grace couldn't put her finger on why she didn't trust Antonio. Everything he'd boasted to them about had proved true. His father had recently passed away leaving him in full control of their family business. What exactly that business was Grace didn't know and was yet to find out. He'd inherited land and property just outside Tivoli where his mother and brother, Roberto lived. He also had an apartment in Rome which was his preferred residence. Even so, Grace's bullshit antennae quivered.

The largest freestanding amphitheatre in the Roman world towered over them. Grace fingered the euro coin in her pocket depicting the Colosseum as it now stood. She watched Antonio and Isobel embrace in a warm hug and hung back a little to give them some space, then veered off to the left and climbed steps to the upper tier and from her vantage point, she looked down. Tourists milling about in the Coliseum's ruins on the ground gave the dark grey blocks of stone colour. Up here alongside Grace, more tourists stood, taking in the impressive scene before them.

Grace lost sight of Isobel and suddenly apprehensive she glanced around in every direction. When at last she spotted them she saw that they were now a trio. A large man had joined them and Antonio seemed to be in an animated conversation with him. Even from this distance, Grace could tell by Isobel's body language that she was uncomfortable. She had stepped away from the two men a few paces and was looking around her as if for help.

Grace took the steps down two at a time. 'Isobel, I'm over here.' Grace called out as she neared. Looking relieved, Isobel walked towards her. 'What's going on, who's that man?' Grace asked.

Isobel shrugged. 'No idea. He's asking Antonio for money he's owed.' Grace and Isobel stood side by side and listened to the heated argument between the two men. Suddenly Antonio held up his hands halting the other man's tirade and spoke in rapid Italian.

'Va bene, Matteo ti darò i soldi, ma prima fammi godermi la mia giornata con Miss Anderson, per favore.'

Whatever Antonio had said satisfied the man, who after a moment of thought walked away.

Antonio walked up to the young women waiting for him. 'I'm going to have to cut short our day out, sorry. Come, I'll take you back to your hotel now.' His voice had an edge to it that neither had heard before.

'I think we can find our way back,' Grace said

looking at Isobel for confirmation.

'Yes, you go Antonio. Grace and I will be fine.' Antonio didn't need telling twice. He turned on his heels and hurried away in the same direction Matteo had gone minutes before.

Grace and Isobel headed back to Piazza Navona and spent time enjoying the small independent shops and boutiques. They watched the world go by while enjoying a coffee in one of the small cafés and Grace decided to approach the subject of Antonio.

'You like him don't you?' she asked.

'What's not to like? He's handsome and rich.' Isobel smiled smugly.

'Has he mentioned to you what business he's in?'

'He deals in art, antiques and antiquities. The same business my father was in and it's how they came to meet. Antonio has contacts all over the world, though. His business is on a completely different level. I never understood how fascinating it is, or how lucrative.'

'Is it all above board, do you think?' Grace probed.

'What do you mean?'

'I can't put my finger on it Isobel, but I don't trust Antonio, and I don't think you should too.'

'Oh, here we go, Grace the sleuth. Have you found a gravestone in the hotel's grounds or a skeleton in the wardrobe? Why are you so suspicious of everyone? Why can't you just enjoy our holiday, and be glad for me? Are you jealous?'

'No, of course, I'm not jealous. I love Jake. But have you forgotten that this visit to Rome was to honour your father's memory? Your father was involved with Antonio and ended up dead.'

'Your right, I'm sorry. Look, we only have a few more days left, so let's make the best of it. I'll be careful I promise. We have our visit to see Inspector Berardi tomorrow. That's not going to be a bundle of fun, is it?'

'Do you still want to go?' Grace was looking forward to it and looked at Isobel hopefully.

'Oh yes. I want to know what my mother was up to while in Rome.'

Detective Inspector Berardi wasn't at all what Grace had expected. She'd pictured him as another Peter Montrose, her sister Amelia's fiancé, but the only thing they had in common was their profession. The Inspector welcomed them by offering coffee and a slice of torte, a flat dense cake stuffed with hazelnuts.

'My wife made it,' he told them proudly.

'Delicious,' Grace said.

'It's very filling.' Isobel took a mouthful and left the rest on her plate.

'So, how can I help you?' Berardi asked.

Before going into the police station, Isobel had pulled Grace to one side. 'Promise me you'll just listen to what the Inspector has to say and leave it to me to ask questions.' Grace promised with her fingers crossed behind her back and now she sat to one side and allowed Isobel to respond.

'Inspector Berardi, my mother told me that when my father's body was recovered from the river, you treated his death as murder. Why was that?'

Berardi leaned forward his arms resting on the desk, hands clasped together. 'Your mother must also have told you that your father was involved in a hit and run a few days before his death.'

'No, I don't remember her mentioning that.' Isobel looked at Grace, who shook her head in reply.

'It was an unfortunate accident that left him with a broken leg and a few broken ribs. Nothing too serious but it did leave him with limited mobility.' Berardi raised his eyebrows and looked from one to the other waiting for the penny to drop.

Grace thought she knew what the inspector was getting at but remained silent. Isobel's expression was blank. 'So,' she said, impatient for him to elaborate.

'Have you been to St Angelo Bridge?'

'Yes, we were there the other day.'

'Did you go down to the towpath? It's there where we believe your father downed.'

'Yes, we did.'

'The steps down are very steep, are they not? Even with two good legs, it would be easy to lose your footing and fall. Only a fool would consider attempting it on crutches.'

Grace couldn't hold her tongue any longer. 'Do you think that's what Mr Anderson did, and then stumbled and fell into the river? That's plausible though, isn't it? So like Isobel said, why a murder inquiry.'

'Isobel glared at her friend. 'Grace, please, you promised me.'

'Your friend makes a good point, Miss Anderson. My first thought was that he'd had assistance, someone who had helped him down and then attacked him. Mr Anderson's crutches had been placed alongside the outer wall of the steps. Who put them there? Surely if he had fallen, they would either be in the river with him or left broken and scuffed on the towpath. We did have a suspect, but we failed to gather any evidence to prove he was in any way responsible for your father's death.'

'Who was the suspect?' Grace asked quickly, ignoring Isobel's glare.

Inspector Berardi smiled at her and shook his head. 'The autopsy on your father's body, Miss Anderson, showed severe injuries, numerous broken bones in addition to his already broken leg. Also, the fact that he had drunk a substantial amount of alcohol before his death explained to everyone's satisfaction the coroner's conclusion. That he had fallen down the steps and in all probability bounced off the towpath and into the river.'

Isobel gulped. She knew the inspector didn't mean to sound indifferent or be insensitive but his bluntness had distressed her. She held her hands to her face as tears fell. 'I don't want to hear anymore.' She sobbed through her fingers.

Grace was by her side in seconds. 'Come on, Isobel, I think you've had enough for one day. Let's go back to the hotel.'

Inspector Berardi stood and escorted them to the door, his expression showing remorse. 'I apologise for my tactlessness,' he said.

Grace hesitated, and Isobel walked on without her. 'Inspector, do you mind if I ask you another question?'

'What is it?'

'Were you satisfied with the coroner's verdict of accidental death?'

'Miss Anderson is very lucky to have you as her friend, Miss Farrell, but please be careful.'

Grace soon caught up with Isobel. She thought about what Inspector Berardi had said. Was it a subtle warning, it had certainly sounded like it?

The next morning over breakfast Isobel made it clear to Grace that she wanted to spend the day with Antonio, without Grace chaperoning her.

'It mustn't be much fun for you trailing along behind us everywhere we go. In any case, Antonio knows that you don't like him. He told me he senses you watching him all the time and your scrutiny makes him feel uncomfortable.'

Grace didn't mind. They were due to fly home the

following day, and she'd decided that another trip to Piazza Navona was due and planned to buy Amelia and Jake a present.

Going through the foyer she noticed Helena and gave her a wave. To Grace's dismay, Helena called to her, so Grace stopped and waited for her.

'Good morning Grace, have you seen my brother this morning by any chance?' Helena said.

'No, he came for Isobel earlier and they've both gone out. Not sure where?'

'Oh!' Helena stood biting her lip and looking anxious.

'Is everything all right?' Grace felt obliged to ask.

'Well no, actually.' Helena hesitated and then decided to explain.' Antonio has decided to sell a few paintings from his collection. I happened to mention it to one of the visitors last night and he's very interested in purchasing the painting Mont Saint Victoire by Paul Cezanne. I messaged Antonio last night and he was supposed to bring the painting here this morning. The thing is, this visitor is due to fly home tomorrow, so it's important he views it today.'

'What are you going to do?' Grace glanced outside longing to breathe in the fresh air and feel the sun on her face.

Helena's face suddenly lit up. 'I have an idea. I have the key to Antonio's apartment here in Rome. It isn't very far, I'll pay for a taxi and it won't take long. I would go myself but there's a tour in half an hour and I need to be here to organise it.'

It took a few moments for Grace to grasp what Helena was getting at. 'Are you asking me to go and get the painting?' she asked, surprised.

'Oh will you, please. The frame it's in isn't big and will probably fit into a large size carrier bag. Hang on I'll go and get the key.' Helena jogged over to reception and retrieved her handbag from behind the counter. She was back beside Grace in a minute. 'Here you are, and this is the address. I've also written down the code you'll need to get through the main door. Antonio's apartment is on the second floor, number twenty-four.' Helena handed Grace a slip of paper and then pushed a wad of euros into her hand. 'This should cover the taxi fare there and back.'

'What does the painting look like? I might bring back the wrong one.'

Helena pulled out her mobile and after a moment of flicking she held it in front of Grace for her to see the picture posted on it. 'Look, a mountain with a landscape of trees in front of it. When you return, take it to your room for safety. Thank you, Grace, I'll see you later. Ciao.'

Grace asked the taxi to wait and let herself into Antonio's apartment building. Once inside number twenty-four, she began her search and soon found the Mont Saint Victoire painting. It was displayed among a variety of ornate framed paintings and which to Grace's uninformed eye looked insignificant beside the larger more detailed artwork.

Grace placed her handbag on one of the sofas and stood in front of it. It was placed high on the wall and although Grace was tall she had to move closer to the wall to get a good stretch. As she did her foot clunked against something on the floor. It was another painting and she crouched down to have a look at it and saw it was a duplicate Mont Saint Victoire. Lifting it she compared the two. 'What the hell,' she muttered, wondering which one she was supposed to take back to Helena.

Noises from outside the apartment door and the

sound of a key in the lock forced her into action. She put the painting back down on the floor and ran into an adjoining room, remembering to pick up her bag. She stood inside what was Antonio's bedroom and listened behind the door. It will most probably be Antonio and Isobel returning to the apartment for lunch, she thought, suddenly feeling silly for hiding. Grace was just about to go back into the sitting room when she heard the loud voices of two men in conversation fill the apartment. After a few minutes, she heard the outside door slam and she breathed a sigh of relief. Grace had envisioned a quick search of the apartment to find out more about Antonio's business but the interruption by the two men had unnerved her and she decided against it. She hurried to the place where the Paul Cezanne paintings were. Above her the original still hung, the duplicate was no longer on the floor.

Outside the taxi had gone. Grace looked up and down the road, not knowing which way she should go. She began walking back the way the taxi had driven and came across a small piazza. On one side trestle tables were laden with various products for sale, cheeses and fresh bread, fruit and vegetables, hand-knitted items, and artisan pots. 'Hotel Muscatello?' she said to one of the store holders, who shook his head at her.

'St. Angelo Bridge?' Grace asked another, who waved his arms pointing up a narrow street leading off the piazza. Grace took this as the way to go and before long she could see touristy signs of life. A café with tables and chairs outside looked inviting and she sat and ordered coffee and thought about the two paintings and what they meant.

When Grace arrived back at the hotel thirty minutes later Helena was still out on the tour. In her room, she began to pack. They were flying home, back to the U.K. tomorrow, and it was a relief. She'd had enough of worrying about Isobel, and Antonio's dubious business. She didn't want to think about the two Cezanne paintings or the men in Antonio's apartment. All she wanted now was to be home with Amelia and see Jake.

CHAPTER 21

Away from David's house and without any particular direction in mind, somehow Vivien's car had brought to her friend and confidante, Amelia Farrell. Not wanting to leave the sanctuary of her car just yet, she sat in the car and looked around. Amelia and her sister, Grace Farrell, their nearest neighbours, lived in Primrose Cottage. Their land joined the rear and east of Mark and Vivien's property but because of the acreage between them, they weren't close. Nevertheless, over the preceding few years, Vivien and Isobel had become friends with the sisters, and Mark had supplied items of furniture to help them get back on their feet after a fire nearly destroyed their Cottage.

The wedding of Amelia and her fiancé, Peter Montrose, a DCI working for the Cheshire constabulary, was set to take place at the end of August. It was the talk of Woodbury village and almost everyone had been invited. Mark had offered to supply the marquee and Vivien's contribution was to help with the flowers. Mrs Brownlow who owned the bakery and ran the little cake shop in Woodbury's high street has offered to make the wedding cake. Not for free mind you, but it was at least one item to tick off the long list of necessities. The service would take place in Woodbury's, St Martin's Church, held by the new vicar, Reverend Reginald Hill. The wedding breakfast, albeit in the late afternoon and carry on until evening, would be held in Primrose Cottage's garden.

Thick trunked oak trees spilt into the garden from Oakham Wood and stood like sentries on guard. Dark shadows flitted between the trees and branches as clouds glided across the sun. Flowering shrubs, hydrangeas and rhododendrons, placed on each side of a wrought iron bench and sheltered under the trees overhanging branches looked inviting. It was hard to believe that less than two years ago, Amelia, and her sister, Grace, had found an old gravestone hidden there. An involuntary shudder brought Vivien back to the matter in hand.

The painting, Boy Peeling Fruit, lay in the boot of her car. It wasn't ideal but the best Vivien could come up with for now. The pressure to confess and unburden her guilt was unbearable. Vivien had to confide in someone and knew she couldn't put it off for much longer. She picked up her handbag and stepped out of the car.

'Is Peter at home?' Vivien asked with her fingers crossed behind her back hoping he wasn't.

Amelia was surprised at Vivien's sudden arrival and directness but made a joke of it. 'Hi Amelia how are you today?' she replied smiling.

'Sorry, how are you, Amelia?' Vivien gave a half-hearted smile in return.

'I'm fine, but it's obvious you're not. Come on in.' Amelia led Vivien into her kitchen. 'Peter's working but if it's important I'll try and get hold of him for you.'

'No don't do that. No need, it's you I've come to see.'

'How about a drink, while we're having a catch-up.'

'Please, as long as it isn't tea or coffee, I need something alcoholic.'

Amelia went to the fridge and pulled out a bottle of Pinot Grigio. 'Who would have thought, readily chilled.'

'Perfect,' sighed Vivien. 'A very small one though,

I'm driving.'

While Amelia poured wine for them both, she said, 'I received a text from Grace last night. She and Isobel are having a great time by the sounds of it. They've met a young man, the brother of the tour guide. I think you know them both. He's been escorting them to all the best places of interest in Rome, and they're enjoying a bit of nightlife too. Three's a crowd and all that but there's safety in numbers right. Come on, we'll be more comfortable in the sitting room.'

Vivien followed and stood by the window mindlessly sipping her drink, again aggrieved that Isobel had chosen not to text her. Amelia was telling her about her latest decorating and soft furnishing contract but her words were of little meaning to Vivien. Under normal circumstances, she would want to see the swatches of fabric Amelia intended to use and know the colours for the walls. Today the only fabric and hues on Vivien's mind were in a painting. Like the soft drape and folds of a boy's shirt, and the different shades of ripe fruit. Vivien concentrated on trying to decide how much she should tell her friend, or if indeed she should say anything at all. As if of their own accord, the words were out of her mouth interrupting Amelia's flow of conversation. 'I've done a terrible thing, Amelia. I want to confide in you but first, will you promise you won't mention what I tell you, to Peter.'

'Come and sit down. You've had a dreadful ordeal. Whatever it is I'm sure it isn't that bad. Mark wasn't the easiest person to be married to I know, even so, it must have been a terrible shock for you.'

'Mark was so charming when we met, and after we married and for the first few years, we were very much in love, well I was. Then we had Isobel and he began to change. I tried my best to come to terms with his darker side, but eventually, I couldn't stand him touching me.'

Vivien said softly. Tears began to slide down her face. Saying it out loud had brought home to her how much of a victim she'd let herself become. Ashamed, she held her hands to her face and quietly sobbed. 'Forgive me. I shouldn't burden you with this.'

'Tell me what's troubling you. You know what they say. A problem shared is a problem halved.' Amelia tried to make light of the situation.

Vivien took another sip of wine and thought about what she wanted Amelia to know, and what she didn't. She took a deep breath and let out a sigh. 'I'm frightened, and I don't know what to do about it. The young man who has befriended Isobel and Grace isn't all he seems. His name is Antonio Cortez. He and Mark had a business deal of sorts involving a stolen painting.'

Amelia stared at Vivien in disbelief. 'You're joking.' Amelia had encouraged Grace to accompany Isobel on her visit to Rome and knew she would never forgive herself, or get over it if anything happened to her sister while she was there. She began to feel alarmed.

Vivien couldn't meet Amelia's eyes as she explained further. 'A few years ago some paintings and sketches were found in derelict churches in Milan and art historians believed them to be early works of students who studied under an artist named Simone Peterzano. A few are believed to be the work of Caravaggio. A painting allegedly stolen from the find in Milan became available on the black market.'

'How is this relevant to Grace and Isobel? Are you saying Antonio stole the painting?'

'I don't know who stole it. Whoever it was, they sold the painting on. Antonio works for the owner and was dealing with the sale. He was Mark's contact in Italy.'

'Good God, the girls are going around with a criminal.' Amelia stood and began to pace. 'What are we going to do?'

Vivien felt guilty. Her concern had been for Isobel but of course, she wasn't the only one who could be in danger. There was Grace to think about too. Before Vivien could say any more, Amelia sat down again.

'You said you'd done something terrible. Is it to do with Antonio? Did you have an affair with him? Considering how Mark treated you, I wouldn't blame you, and finding out he's now befriended Isobel is bound to upset you. Are you worried in case Antonio tells her about you and him?'

'Oh Amelia, If only it was as simple as that.' Vivien shook her head and for the first time that day, she felt like laughing and did. Vivien thought about Jack and blushed. She hadn't seen him or heard from him since her return to Woodbury. She wished she could tell Amelia about him and the whole sorry story. 'I didn't have an affair with Antonio, no.'

'What is it then? Are you going to tell me or not?'

'Can I trust you not to say anything about all this to Peter? What I tell you is in strict confidence and can't go any further.' The last thing Vivien wanted was for DCI Peter Montrose to be involved.

'I don't keep secrets from Peter but as long as you haven't done anything illegal, I'll make an exception. So yes, you can trust me.'

'That's just it, I have but I have got to tell someone soon otherwise I may go out of my mind.'

'Go on, then.' Amelia took hold of Vivien's hand for encouragement.

'Antonio was arrested in connection to Mark's death but later after the coroner announced his death accidental, Antonio was released from prison.

'You said earlier that you were frightened. Who of, Antonio? Surely if the police let him go they had no evidence, and so he's no threat to you or the girls now.'

'Then why did he search out Isobel. Why is he

spending so much time with her? I believe the deal he made with Mark didn't go through as planned and now he's using my daughter to get to me.'

'I still don't understand where you come into this, Vivien. It just doesn't add up, that's all. I gather you're worried Antonio will come after you, but for what?'

'The owner hasn't been paid for the painting. If not Antonio, he'll send someone else for the money Mark owes.'

'So you think Antonio is dangerous?'

'Yes I do, I'm sure of it.'

'If that's the case, I'm really worried about Grace. Once she gets a sniff of something dodgy she'll be poking her nose in, and where that will lead to heaven knows. Amelia became quiet while she drained the rest of her wine. 'I think there's more to it. Something you're not telling me. How come you know about a deal Antonio had with Mark. From what I've learned in the past it seems unlikely to me that Mark would confide in you or involve you in any business deal, dodgy or not.'

'You're beginning to sound like your husband,' Vivien replied, uncomfortable with Amelia's questions.

'Who has the painting now then?'

'I have it, Amelia.'

'You?' Visions of her friend dressed in a black cat-suit, black eye mask, and climbing through windows filled Amelia's mind and she shook her head. 'I read an old newspaper article a couple of months ago, about a Caravaggio painting at a Sotheby's auction in 2001. Experts attributed the picture as "Circle of Caravaggio" and it was worth millions.'

'Don't forget, this painting hasn't been authenticated yet, so it may not be by Caravaggio, and therefore worthless. Although if you saw it, the detail and colour, well it's hard to believe it could have been painted by anyone else.'

'How come you've got it and more to the point, what are you going to do with it?' Amelia asked.

'I hoped you'd tell me that. Antonio is ingratiating himself on Isobel to get to me for the payment, or the painting.'

'And you're not prepared to pay him, or give him the painting?

'What? Why should I pay him, and in any case I don't have that kind of money going spare? The painting doesn't belong to him, fake or otherwise. Are you saying that's what I should do?'

'It's the easiest solution and have you forgotten, the painting doesn't belong to you either.'

'But he's a criminal, Amelia. I would be aiding and abetting, or whatever Peter calls it.'

'I understand now why you don't want me to tell Peter. You know what he would say don't you?' Amelia took a deep breath. 'I'm going to make us a coffee, we need caffeine. Think about what you just said while I've gone.'

The last thing Amelia wanted was to get involved in another crisis but knew Grace would jump at the chance. They had only recently fully recovered from the trauma she and Grace had suffered eighteen months ago. An inheritance had brought them to Woodbury to live in a lovely old cottage with a large garden next to fields and woodland. Sadly it wasn't all they inherited. Not long after they'd moved in, Grace found a gravestone in the garden and both their lives had been turned upside down. Further inspection, insisted on by Grace, had them unearthing a coffin containing the bones of a young girl and her baby. Unfortunately for them, they also unearthed a long-buried secret. The consequence of that was something she was trying hard to forget. Gossiping in the village was rampant causing her decorating and soft furnishing business to suffer, and subsequently, take a downward turn. Her reputation had suffered when she hadn't been able to complete orders or commit to deadlines, and so her customers had taken their business elsewhere. It all resulted in them having to sell their shop in Llangollen, including the one-bedroomed flat above. Gwyneth her assistant and friend had lived in the flat for many years and it would have broken her heart to leave, had it not been for Joe Jones, Amelia and Grace's gardener. Gwyneth and Joe had hit it off on their first meeting and over the following months, their friendship blossomed. When Amelia told Gwyneth that the shop and flat had to be sold, it seemed natural for her to move in with Joe. The equity from the sale had enabled Amelia to have a large log cabin built in the garden. The cabin was where she now ran her business, with plenty of room for her sewing machine, cutting table and fabrics store. They had been able to renovate the cottage after a fire had almost destroyed it, and Amelia looked around her new kitchen with pride.

Vivien sat in Amelia's sitting room waiting for her coffee. Even though she'd been stunned by Amelia's outlook on the problem, Vivien knew it was true. She was no better than Antonio. Giving the painting back to Antonio was the easiest option. But how could she be sure that would be the end of it. Antonio could use it to blackmail her. No, she couldn't do it, she wouldn't. Her instinct told her to either take the painting to the Galleria in Rome or give it back to Jack.

Amelia returned with two steaming mugs of coffee and a plate of scones. She cut a scone in half and buttered it. A worried look creased her brow and her smile was gone. She sat down beside Vivien. 'Well?'

'You're right. I've decided that when Isobel and Grace return, I shall book a flight to Rome and take the painting to the Galleria.'

'Good. Would you like me to come with you?'

'No, it is something I must do by myself. Anyway, it might make Peter suspicious and I really would prefer he didn't know.'

'I won't breathe a word,' Amelia said, with her fingers crossed behind her back.

CARAVAGGIO: IN THE CITY OF NAPLES AND ON HIS WAY BACK TO ROME

1609-1610

The customary term of exile was three years and so now Caravaggio hoped he would receive a pardon. His enemies hadn't forgiven him though or given up searching for him. They eventually found him in Osteria Del Cerriglio, a tavern in which Caravaggio frequented. The attack was brutal and Caravaggio's injuries were severe, so much so, a newspaper article sent word of his death to Rome. The wounds inflicted on his face left him badly scarred, almost unrecognisable.

During his slow recovery and convalescence, Caravaggio began a series of smaller paintings. These he sent to Rome in the hope that he might gain favour and at last, he was granted an official pardon. In the summer of 1610, Caravaggio began his journey back to Rome and in Chiaia he boarded a large felucca. He took with him several paintings, some intended for Cardinal Scipione Borghese.

Dalmazio, the felucca's captain, stood leaning over the rail and watched the painter called Caravaggio come aboard. He carried with him a stack of canvases rolled and tied securely. Dalmazio shouted orders and two barefoot deckhands wearing ankle-length pants and checked linen shirts scurried down to the key side. Breathing heavily each one heaved aboard a leather trunk. The largest man, Taddeo, ran back to carry on a third smaller trunk and this he placed at Caravaggio's feet with the others.

As the boat slipped out of the dock and met the choppy Mediterranean waters the ship's brass lamps swayed and clunked against a beam. Brown hessian sacking lay in folds on the deck, some placed on benches where passengers might sit. The wooden vessel didn't have cabins, and so Caravaggio sat on one of his large trunks to rest during the journey. The few other passengers on board avoided him, having already heard of his quarrelsome reputation.

On the way to Rome, the felucca put in at Palo, a Tuscany port. Palo was under Spanish control and ominously the vessel was detained. Caravaggio disembarked and was held for questioning. Still suffering from his recent injuries he asked to be allowed to book into the small hotel while the captain checked his credentials and validated his pardon. The captain of the fortress castle on Palo refused and put Caravaggio in a cold damp prison.

While Caravaggio was detained the tide turned, and Dalmazio set sail without him, taking all of Caravaggio's luggage and paintings.

Two days later, Caravaggio managed to buy his way out of prison. Finding the felucca gone he became enraged and desperate. He hired a small boat to chase after it but that failed. Caravaggio then made the fateful decision to walk along the scalding beach and catch up with the ship farther up the coast. He got as far as Port' Ercole where he collapsed and died of fever in the small infirmary run by the brothers of San Sebastian.

Everyone of importance in Rome was waiting for Caravaggio, and the unbelievable news of his death sped fast. A document granting him clemency arrived from the Pope in Rome, three days after his death.

CHAPTER 22

As a peace offering, David offered to collect Isobel and Grace from the airport on the day of their return. Vivien was still smarting over his disloyalty so she refused. In any case, she needed to do it. It was the first time Isobel had been away from home and Vivien wanted to give her the welcome back she deserved, after losing her father in such dreadful circumstances. She hoped that now there was going to be just the two of them, they could put past hurt behind them and draw closer together as mother and daughter should be.

Vivien arrived at Manchester airport in plenty of time, parked her car and retrieved a parking ticket from the machine. There was ample time to waste so she bought a coffee and settled down to wait where she could keep my eye on the arrivals screen and doors. The flight was on time and the luggage must have been unloaded in record time, because before Vivien knew it there they were, waving in the distance. Vivien smiled happily and waved back. Isobel and Grace rushed towards her.

'Oh Mum, I had a fantastic time.' Isobel exclaimed hugging her.

'I'm glad you're both home safe.' Vivien slipped her arm around Grace's waist to include her in the conversation. Looking down and about them, she saw they had no luggage with them. 'Where are your cases?

Have you forgotten to pick them up?'

'Antonio's collecting them so that we could come straight through and find you. Wait until you meet him, Mum, he's gorgeous isn't he, Grace?' Grace shrugged, her expression non-committal. 'Here he is now, let me introduce you.'

Antonio appeared pushing a trolley with three suitcases and carry-on bags loaded onto it. Grinning he walked towards them. 'Bon journo, Vivien, we meet again.'

Isobel looked from one to the other confused. 'Do you two already know each other?'

Vivien was so shocked to see Antonio it took her a few minutes to reply. She just nodded and began to walk towards the exit. Isobel, Grace, and Antonio followed. 'Not really,' she said eventually. 'We met when I visited the Trevi Fountain on one of the tours.'

'Yes, I remember, a beautiful day wasn't it?' Antonio called to her.

Vivien paid for her parking at one of the machines ignoring any attempt at the conversation the others tried to make. She was furious with Isobel for bringing Antonio back to the UK with her and she remained silent on their journey home.

When they arrived at Primrose Cottage to drop Grace off, Amelia stood at the door and waved to them. Vivien half-heartedly waved back. Grace rushed into the arms of Jake who held a large bouquet of cream roses.

After Vivien had reversed the car and directed it towards home, Isobel excitedly told Vivien about the wonderful places she had visited. Antonio chimed in now and again to correct her pronunciation of Italian names. Vivien only managed a quiet mumble in response and the conversation soon became stilted. From her occasional glance in the review mirror, Vivien could see Antonio's self-satisfied face sneering back at her.

Still unable to come to terms that Antonio, the man who had instigated a vicious attack on her husband, was here in her house, she left Isobel to show Antonio around and walked over to the barn needing to be alone. She sat in the office, her head in her hands wondering how she was going to cope with this new worry.

Full of enthusiasm, Isobel showed Antonio around the house. Vivien had insisted he sleep in the guest room and after he'd dumped his case and a scruffy black backpack on the bed, Isobel showed him her room. Along the landing next to the main bathroom was the master bedroom where Vivien now slept alone. Isobel took Antonio in there and knelt on a window seat built into the bay window. She began to point out the summer house in the pretty landscaped garden, the little orchard placed just to the right, where, in the autumn they would be able to pick the apples, and her mother, Vivien, would make pies.

'On the far side at the edge of the land is a lake, well more like a large pond really,' Isobel told him. With her back to Antonio, she happily went on to explain how the business was conducted next door in the large barn. 'It's like an Aladdin's cave in there. Some rooms haven't seen the light of day since the stuff was moved in. Dad was always saying he was going to do an itinerary of everything and have a kind of a rotation system of items to display. I don't think he ever got round to it.' The last sentence was said sadly, and she turned to see if Antonio was listening.

While Isobel had been prattling on Antonio had taken the opportunity to have a good look around the room. He deftly lifted the edges of several paintings hanging on the walls to check if they hid the painting, Boy Peeling Fruit, or a safe. The fitted wardrobes were built up to the ceiling he noticed, but there was plenty of room inside to hide something, he thought. He smiled at Isobel when he noticed her looking at him and went to sit by her on the window seat. Isobel immediately put herself on his knees and placed her arms around his neck then kissed him softly on his mouth.

Antonio responded, the gentle kisses becoming more urgent. 'Let's get more comfortable,' he whispered through a tangle of Isobel's long hair. He began to lead her over towards the grand queen-sized bed.

'No, we can't, not here.' Isobel tried to pull him over to the door.

'Vivien's gone in the barn. She'll be a while yet. Come on Issy, live dangerously for once.' Antonio encouraged. It took seconds for Isobel to shed her clothes and climb into bed beside Antonio who'd wasted no time making himself at home. Antonio took her into his arms and kissed her passionately. He found the young women's pale soft flesh irresistible.

Isobel had never met anyone like Antonio before, so handsome and experienced. The few boyfriends she'd had up until now she'd found immature. She realised she preferred an older man and was flattered that Antonio wanted her and found her sexy. They enjoyed each other's body and Isobel happily succumbed to his every need.

When Vivien returned to the house about forty-five minutes later, she called out to Isobel to let her know she was back. When no reply came she assumed the two of them had gone out for a walk. She decided to make use of some quiet time and take a refreshing shower. When Vivien entered her bedroom, the first thing she noticed was that her bed was unmade. Positive she'd made her bed before leaving for the airport she stood for a moment frowning. While she undressed she heard the sound of laughter close by and she slipped on her dressing gown. The sound was coming from the wardrobe. Before she reached it and had time to turn the handle, the doors opened and a naked Isobel rushed out. She disappeared onto the landing heading no doubt to her bedroom. Open-mouthed, Vivien watched Antonio follow her, his taut naked white bottom in stark contrast to his suntanned legs and back. Vivien clasped her hands to her mouth. Horrified and appalled she walked over to the window seat and sat down, shaken.

Vivien knew it was up to her to protect her daughter no matter what, and so gradually as the minutes ticked by and the sky darkened, Vivien began to make plans. She wasn't going to let Antonio ruin Isobel or her future.

Antonio had made it clear from the start that his stay would be temporary. Isobel had pouted and tried to persuade him to delay his return but after a week it was clear he was getting restless. On a few occasions, Vivien caught him alone in various rooms of the house. When she'd disturbed him he had given her some lame reason for being there. Paintings on the walls were askew. Drawers had not been closed properly. Her clothes were pushed to one side of the rail in her wardrobe, and her shoe boxes shifted, lids out of line. Vivien had thought Antonio would come after her for the missing Euro's Mark owed, and the painting, but that didn't make sense. Why would he want a forged painting? Perhaps because it was evidence the police could use against his deceased father? Was it to protect his father's reputation and his family, including himself, from prosecution.

Antonio rarely slept in the guest room allocated for him. Vivien didn't approve of the accommodating way Isobel was with him, allowing him to sleep in her room night after night but what could she do. It was what Isobel wanted. She was eighteen, a young woman, and if anything like her father, well, enough said.

Antonio's presence in the house unnerved Vivien. She couldn't bear the thought of him roaming around in the middle of the night rummaging through her belongings so she didn't sleep well. At the beginning of the second week of Antonio's stay, Vivien decided to go to bed early. Emotionally drained, her nerves jagged and raw, she fell asleep almost immediately. She woke sometime later with a sudden start. Something, a noise, had disturbed her and she lay listening. The alarm clock glowed two forty-five a.m. The sound of a low cough had her sitting upright and she cried out in fright at the sight of Antonio standing by the side of her bed. He clamped his hand over her mouth to stop her from screaming.

'Shut up,' he snarled in her ear.

Wide-eyed and terrified Vivien complied. Her breathing gradually began to slow but she couldn't stop trembling. At last, Antonio removed his hand from her mouth and clutched her wrist tightly instead. He sat beside her on the edge of the bed.

'What have you done with it?' he asked her.

'What?'

'The money you took from the locker. You think you are very clever, don't you, Vivien.'

'No.' The word came out in a squeak.

'The key you gave to your husband wasn't the key Caplan gave you, was it?'

'No, that key was stolen from me. I had to have another key cut to give to Mark. He had a vicious temper and I was frightened of him, and what he might do if I returned with nothing to give him.' Vivien spoke quietly, not wanting to wake Isobel.

'Stolen by whom?'

'A man helped me after I was mugged, he took it.'

'I don't believe you.' Antonio gripped Vivien's wrist

tighter, and she winced.

'You went to the Rail Terminal and emptied the locker, and Mark used the key I gave him to retrieve the painting. Nice little con you had going on there. Quiet little mouse Vivien, who would have thought it. Well just so you know I'm not leaving until I get what I'm owed.'

'I'm not lying. The man who took the key works for customs and excise, his name is Jack Tyler. He stole the key from me the night I went to see Caplan. He forced me to go with him to the Rail Terminal and tell him the number of the locker the key opened. He has the money, not me.'

'So, you're on first name terms with Tyler. I should have known you'd give in easily to his pressure. You don't need to be frightened of Mark anymore do you, he's dead but I'm not. It's me you should be worried about now, and what I might do.'

'I am frightened, Antonio.'

'When my men left Mark on the towpath he was very much alive but you know that don't you? You were there on the bridge, they saw you. Berardi was very interested when I told him.'

Vivien gulped. If the police had known all along she was there at the time of Mark's death, why hadn't she been called to give evidence against Antonio? Perhaps he hadn't believed Antonio or was it just easier for Inspector Berardi to call it an accident and close the case. Vivien was confused. 'Mark was in a bad way when I found him. I went for help,' she said after a moment.

'Who has the painting?'

'Mark gave it to me to carry for him after we met at the Terminal.'

'So you have it, I thought as much. The painting belonged to my father and it meant a great deal to him. I want it back, so where is it?'

'Jack took it from me.'

'If Tyler has the money and the painting it means we gained nothing from the arrangement we made with your husband. If you value your daughter's life as well as your own, you're going to pay us everything my family is owed.'

'I haven't got that kind of money.'

'I think you have, and you have until the end of this week to get it.'

CHAPTER 23

The next morning Antonio acted as if nothing had happened. Vivien might have thought she had dreamt it if it wasn't for the bruising around her left wrist. He sat eating his breakfast and making small talk with Isobel.

'Antonio and I are going into Chester for the day, Mum. We're going to the cinema later, so Antonio has booked us in for a night at the Travelodge on Little St John Street. We won't be back until tomorrow morning.'

'I hope you have a nice time,' Vivien answered without meaning it. She didn't like the idea of Isobel spending the night in a hotel with Antonio but didn't say.

'Is it okay if we take Dad's car?'

Vivien was grateful she was standing at the sink facing the kitchen window with her back to Isobel. After her return from her visit to Amelia Farrell, she had transferred the stolen painting into the boot of Mark's Mercedes which was no longer being used. In the antique barn, she had found three framed oil paintings of similar size and little value. She placed the Boy Peeling Fruit canvas on top of one of the paintings and then wrapped them all individually in brown paper and string. The three packages she put into the boot of Mark's car laying one on top of the other, as though Mark had prepared them ready for delivery after he'd returned from holiday. There was no way she could allow Isobel and Antonio the keys to Mark's car.

Vivien walked over to a basket on the dresser where all their keys were thrown until needed. She picked up the Mercedes car keys and slipped them into her skirt pocket and then turned to face Isobel. Holding out the keys to her own smaller Volkswagen, she said. 'I should have mentioned it. I've advertised your father's car for sale and I have someone coming this afternoon to look at it. Why don't you take my car instead?'

Within ten minutes Vivien heard the sound of her car accelerating away and she immediately picked up the telephone and pressed David Lanceley's number. He answered on the third ring.

'Hello, David it's me, Vivien.'

'Hi Viv, we must be telepathic, I was just going to ring you,' he told her. 'Are you friends with me now? You rushed off in a bit of a huff the other day.'

'I don't like it when you keep secrets from me, especially when it's to do with Isobel. She's my daughter, David, not yours.'

'I'm sorry, it won't happen again.'

Vivien took a deep breath. 'You can make it up to me by doing me a favour.'

'I will if I can.'

'Is it okay if I park Mark's car in your garage? It will only be for a week or two.'

'You have a double garage right next to the barn.'

'I know. But I want the car away from the house. I'll explain when I see you.'

'I'll have to park my Jaguar on the drive instead of in my garage. I'm not happy to do that.'

'Where is it parked now?'

'Err, on the driveway.'

'I'll see you in twenty minutes, bye.'

When Vivien arrived at David's he had thoughtfully park his Jaguar on the street in front of his house. The garage door was open and Vivien drove the Mercedes straight in. It was a tight squeeze but she managed to get out of the car without scraping the door. David came out of the house and drove his car back onto the drive.

'Do you have the key? It's an expensive car and I would feel happier if your garage is locked.' Vivien told him.

David sighed and locked his garage door. Inside the house, David made tea and put a few biscuits on a plate. 'I might be interested in buying Mark's car, you know. I've always admired it. How much do you want for it?'

'I need to check the current market value. Perhaps you could do that for me?' Vivien suggested, dunking a biscuit.

'I will. Now, tell me the real reason Mark's car is parked in my garage.'

'You know Antonio Cortez is staying with us.'

'Yes, I must admit I was surprised to hear he travelled from Rome with Isobel and Grace. Even more surprised you allowed him to stay at Lilac House.'

'I'm not happy about it but I didn't have a choice. Isobel is so infatuated with him she would give him the moon if she could reach it. Mark's car on the other hand is more easily accessible. I don't trust him, David, and the car won't be here for long, I promise.'

David understood to some extent her unease about Antonio, so he didn't question Vivien further. Besides, there was something else they needed to discuss.

'Vivien, there is something you need to know. Please don't be angry when I tell you. Mark borrowed money from me to pay for his Caravaggio. I didn't know all the details at the time. He told me it was for an investment similar to mine, in a property. My bank advised I insist on some sort of surety for the loan and Mark signed a quarter of Anderson Antiques over to me. He assured me that the loan was temporary and would be paid back in a few months. We shook hands with the understanding that my claim on the barn would then be made null and void.'

Vivien listened to David, taking in his words but not quite understanding what they meant.

'I promise I won't interfere in any way, unless you want me to, of course. What do I know about antiques?' David laughed trying to ease the tension. Vivien's face had gone pale and she looked near to tears. 'You know you can trust me, Vivien. Please don't be upset.'

'How much did Mark borrow from you?'

'It was a hundred thousand pounds.'

Vivien accepted what David had told her. What bothered her though was where Mark had found the remaining money. She couldn't envisage a business partnership with David but had no means in which to pay him off. She finished her tea and stood ready for David to drive her home. Neither spoke on the journey.

David dropped Vivien off at the end of her driveway and on his way back to Lower Shelton; he pulled into the side of the road and made a call.

Jack Tyler answered straight away.

'Hi, Jack it's David.'

'What have you got for me?'

'I don't know if it means anything but Vivien brought Mark's car round to my house today. She almost insisted I let her park it in my garage.'

'Did she say why?' Jack asked. He was sat at his desk in his office studying the insufficient evidence he had on the deceased Alonzo Cortez, and his family.

'Yes, she's thinking of selling it. Plus, she's worried Antonio will get his hands on it. The thing is Jack, there's a double garage at Lilac House. Why didn't she lock it in one of those?'

'Did you agree?' Attentive, Jack shifted in his chair.

'Yes. It's safely locked in my garage and I kept the

key. I don't have the keys to the Mercedes though. I'm thinking of buying the car from her, actually.'

'Did you tell her that?'

'Yes.'

'Good. Ask Vivien if you can take it out for a test drive and let me know when you've arranged it for. I'll come to Lower Shelton as soon as you know. I need to take a look inside that car.'

CHAPTER 24

After the film and a few drinks in the Ye Olde King's Head Pub, on Lower Bridge Street, Isobel and Antonio booked into the Travelodge. While Isobel unpacked the few toiletries she'd brought with her, Antonio made a call on his mobile. It was nine forty-five, still early evening but Isobel was ready to call it a night. All she wanted to do was snuggle up in bed with Antonio, relax and maybe watch a film on television. Antonio had another agenda.

'Shall we go down to the bar and have a nightcap before we turn in?' he said.

'Do you mind if we don't?' Isobel replied.

'Well, I need a cigarette before I call it a night, so I'm going. You'll be alright here on your own while I'm away, won't you?'

'Yes, of course. Please, don't be too long, though.' Isobel replied wistfully.

Outside the hotel, Antonio lit a cigarette and inhaled deeply. It had grown cooler now and clouds had begun to gather. The hotel was near Chester's Roman Amphitheatre and Antonio crossed the road to get a better view of its size. It had upper tiers of seats via stairs on the rear wall and a small shrine near the north entrance. Antonio thought it ironic that he, an Italian, was looking at something his countrymen had built centuries ago, in another country, an island, with so diverse a culture. Everything about Chester spoke of its Roman ancestry. The Roman walls surrounding the city, Ruins of a Roman garden where he'd watched students eat their lunch earlier that day. He'd read somewhere that originally Chester had been a Roman fort named Deva Victrix.

Antonio looked at his watch. He'd arranged to meet Julie Merriton near the entrance to Chester's Grosvenor Park and he was late. He hurried for the rest of the short way unconsciously rubbing his hands together as if preparing them, and himself, for what they were about to do.

Julie stood waiting for Antonio by a bus shelter. She was quite tall and looked elegant dressed in a green floral dress with a cream coloured jacket over it. Around her neck, a knotted pink scarf was draped across her chest.

'Is that you, Antonio,' Julie asked, as Antonio drew closer.

'Mi dispiace tanto sono in ritardo,' he replied.

'No idea what you just said,' Julie retorted, laughing. 'Let's stick to English shall we?'

'I'm so sorry I'm late. Thank you for waiting.' The entrance to Grosvenor Park was a few metres away and Antonio began to walk towards it. 'Shall we find somewhere quiet to sit? We have a lot to discuss.'

Julie followed Antonio as he knew she would. He was surprised by how thin she was. Even her sandals seemed too big and they clonked on the path as she walked along beside him.

While they walked, Julie chatted. 'I was shocked when I heard about Alonzo's heart attack, Antonio, and then what happened to poor Mark. I was so upset. I feel as though Mark's death is my fault, you know. If I hadn't involved him in our deal, he would still be alive. I had to go to London on business after he and his wife left for Rome. When I returned home I found numerous messages on my answer machine from him. He was concerned about you mainly and wanted to know if you were the contact he was supposed to meet.'

They had reached the main wider lane that ran the full length of the park. Small narrower paths haphazardly branched off in different directions. Some led to the Groves and the River Dee. One path led to gardens laid out specifically for the blind. Another path led towards a small pond where ducks swam. Along this main stretch of walkway tall cone-shaped holly trees grew. They were spaced evenly with benches in-between for people to sit and rest. Antonio stopped beside one of the benches and sat down. Julie followed suit.

'Mark's death wasn't your fault, Julie. You didn't force him to get involved. He wanted a Caravaggio and would have done anything to get it.' Antonio told her.

'So, what went wrong? One of Mark's messages said the transaction was to take place via the exchange of keys. He said he had nothing to show for the diamonds he'd taken to the jeweller.'

'You ask me what went wrong, well just about everything. Mark double-crossed us. I gave him the location of the painting and he gave me the key supposedly to a locker containing the payment. Foolishly I trusted him. The locker number didn't exist and even if it had, the key wouldn't have fitted. He was much cleverer than we gave him credit for. Now we are left with nothing, and that's not good. You can imagine, Julie, I'm not happy. Neither would my father be if he were still alive.'

'Why would Mark do that? I've known him a long time and he wasn't that kind of person, Antonio.'

'Mark was a coward, for a start. He made his wife take the diamonds to Caplan. Did you know he abused his wife? Not just emotionally but physically too. I've seen the bruises. A man like that is capable of anything.'

'No, I didn't know that.'

'You say Mark wasn't the kind of person to double-cross, which makes me believe he was working with someone else and this other person put the idea into his head. We've had another Custom and Excise investigator in Rome poking about asking questions and I know for a fact Mark spoke to him. Do you know anything about that Julie?'

'Me, don't be ridiculous.'

'Unfortunately, because of Vivien's involvement and interference, Custom and Excise have the Caravaggio painting, and the money we should have been paid. It's quite a dilemma, don't you agree?'

'I complied with every instruction your father insisted on. I also brought Mark into this so that Alonzo could dupe him into buying one of his fake paintings. As for Mark, he wouldn't do anything to jeopardise him owning a Caravaggio.' Julie didn't like Antonio's change in attitude or the threatening tone to his voice. The park was empty and full of dark shadows so feeling vulnerable she began to stand. Antonio placed his hand on her arm to stop her. 'Let me go, I'm not listening to any more of this,' Julie said, beginning to get upset.

'You're not being very cooperative are you?' Antonio looked at the silk scarf wrapped around Julie's neck. He'd brought a knife with him to do the job but how would he explain to Isobel the splashes of blood on his clothing. No, that would be too messy. Antonio leaned forward towards Julie and gently fingered the scarf around her neck. 'This is pretty,' he said. Slowly he began to wrap the ends of the scarf around each of his hands. He took a glance around to make sure there was no one about to witness his actions.

Julie felt the scarf tighten and lifted her hand to her throat to loosen it. 'You're hurting me, stop it,' she croaked as the scarf tightened.

Antonio was strong and it took little effort to pull and pull harder. A few minutes later Julie's head lolled back against the back of the bench. He shook the scarf away from his hands and stood, then began to make his way out of the park taking an alternative route back towards the main road. He walked slowly and lit a cigarette; the nicotine flare was just what he needed.

CHAPTER 25

Early the following morning, Vivien spent time in the office, checking invoices and accounts on the laptop. Isobel and Antonio hadn't returned home from their night away yet, and she assumed they were going to spend another day in the city. About eleven-thirty, feeling hungry and needing a drink, she made her way back to the house. At the sound of footsteps on the gravel, she turned and watched Detective Chief Inspector Peter Montrose making his way towards her. He'd parked his car where Mark's had been the day before. He smiled as he drew nearer.

'Amelia asked me to look in on you. She said you were a bit distraught the last time she saw you.'

'I'm fine now, thank you. Everything was getting on top of me, you know, Mark's death in Rome, and his funeral.' Amelia had promised not to say anything, and Vivien felt let down. She wondered how much his wife had told him.

'Would you mind if we went inside, this isn't only a social call?'

Vivien's mind raced through all the possibilities for his visit as she walked the rest of the way to the house. She unlocked the door and led Peter into the sitting room. 'Would you like a coffee,' she asked.

'No, thank you.' Peter replied and sat down on one of the leather sofas. Vivien sat on the sofa facing him and waited. 'Late last night a woman was found murdered in Grosvenor Park. This morning, during our search of her apartment, we came across some information concerning

Mark. Your husband's name has cropped up several times during our initial investigation.'

'Mark?' Vivien looked shocked.

'Have you ever heard him mention the name Julie Merriton?'

Vivien felt nauseous. She always did when her nerves got the better of her. 'Yes, Mark had a brief fling with her years ago, long before we met. She's in the antique business too.'

'Did he mention her more recently, say within the last two months?'

'Can I ask how she died?' Vivien enquired, attempting to delay her answer. She could feel her heart speeding up.

'I'm not at liberty to give out that sort of information,' Peter told her flatly. 'Please, answer my questions and then I can let you get on with your day.'

'When Julie found out we were going on holiday to Rome, she asked Mark to take a package and deliver it to a contact she knew over there.' Vivien noticed Peter had begun to take notes.

'What was in the package, do you know?'

'Yes, but is that relevant?'

Peter let out a breath and looked at her steadily. 'It might be, Vivien. I need to glean as much information as possible about the victim.'

'The package contained uncut diamonds. Julie assured Mark it was quite legal to take them out of the country and into Italy. At least while we're still in the EU.'

'Who did Mark deliver them to?'

'I don't know, sorry. Are you sure you wouldn't like coffee? I'm going to make one for myself.'

Peter followed her into the kitchen. 'You have a young man staying with you; the one Isobel and Grace met while in Rome. Is he staying long?' he asked.

'His name is Antonio Cortez. He asked if he could

stay until the end of this week. Isobel likes him so she'll be sad to see him go.'

'What about you?'

'Me? I need to start concentrating on the business again, and there are a few changes I'd like to make in the house. All difficult to do when you have a visitor staying. How are the wedding arrangements coming along?' Vivien attempted to change the subject.

'Amelia has everything in hand. She's very chilled about the whole thing. That reminds me. The marquee Mark promised to provide. We don't expect it now Vivien. I will sort that out.'

'Mark paid for it and arranged the delivery before we went on holiday. It was our wedding gift, after all, so please let it stay that way.'

'If you're sure then,' Peter replied looking relieved, thinking it one less job for him. He didn't indicate that he was ready to leave so Vivien mentioned the weather, asked about Grace and Jake and pointed out the lawn that needed mowing. It was small talk to fill in the awkward silences.

'While Antonio's here get him to mow it,' Peter suggested.

'Good idea,' Vivien said, knowing she would never ask Antonio to do anything for her.

'I'll be on my way then. Thank you for your help, Vivien. If you think of anything else relating to Julie and Mark's relationship, you will let me know, won't you? I'll see myself out.' Vivien stood and watched him from the kitchen window walking towards his car.

DCI Montrose's office was small, made smaller by bookshelves secured against two walls. The large oak desk and tan leather swivel chair took up the remaining space. In and Out trays, a landline, and a framed photo of Amelia adorned the right side of his desk. Cardboard files lay in chaotic piles on his left. In front of him a file containing the information they had compiled on the Julie Merriton murder inquiry. Montrose read through the statements and notes he and his sergeant had made, for the second time that day.

Julie Merriton had been a prodigious wealthy woman, liked by the people that knew her. Business colleagues in the arts and antiquities industry were full of praise, and no one could think of any reason why she had been murdered.

Montrose was inclined to believe that Julie knew her attacker. She'd faced him while he had squeezed the life from her. There were no defence marks for one thing, except bruising to the fingers of her right hand, so she hadn't put up much of a fight. The fingerprints forensics had found on her handbag and its contents proved to be only her own. There were no car keys so she had walked the short distance from her apartment to the park. Only one of Julie's sandals was still attached to a foot, a medium heeled flimsy affair with a strap to hold her toes in place. The other had later been found nearby in a hollowed Holly tree, most likely taken there by a stray animal, squirrel, or cat. Montrose pondered possibilities. He was assuming the murder had been carried out by a man and yet there was no evidence to say it couldn't just as easily have been a woman. They'd found a book, a diary of sorts, during their search of her apartment which showed dates and times of appointments with numerous men. Quite a long line of them, Mark Anderson included.

A jealous wife or girlfriend seeking revenge maybe but Montrose wasn't sold on that idea. Women didn't normally go in for strangulation as a means to kill. There were numerous reasons for a murder of this sort, including mistaken identity, revenge, adultery and greed. His gut ruled out mistaken identity. Again he considered revenge. What had she done in her past so terrible that only death sufficed to satisfy? Up to now, no relatives had come forward to report a missing, sister, mother, or friend? That didn't mean there weren't any siblings. Montrose scribbled a note on his writing pad, a reminder for Fielding to look into it and to check who benefited from her death.

Julie had worn makeup that evening; her hair freshly washed and styled. It indicated she'd gone out to meet someone, a man, on a date perhaps? She would have entered the park if her destination had been, The Boathouse Inn, which stood on the banks of the River Dee. It had riverside rooms with splendid views. Chester's Old Dee Bridge for instance with its Victorian street lamps lighting up the road crossing over the River Dee into a suburb known as Handbridge. It's likely the park would have been empty except for the odd drug taker. Or a tramp that might have been seeking a night's shelter, hidden away from prying eyes underneath one of the numerous benches dotted around the park. Had Julie been in the wrong place at the wrong time? Montrose scribbled another note for his sergeant.

Ms Merriton's body had been found by a newly married couple walking through the park after leaving The Boathouse at eleven p.m. It was the husband who had notified the police after his wife had gone into hysterics at the sight of Julie's propped body on a bench with glazed eyes, tongue protruding and her legs spread.

A knock on his office door aroused Montrose from his musings. Sergeant Robert Fielding entered with a smile on his face.

'Are you ready Sir?' he asked with a grin.

'Oh god is it that time already?' Montrose shuddered.

'Yes, it is,' Fielding replied, glancing at his watch. 'I'll see you downstairs in the car park.' Fielding gave Montrose a mock salute and left.

Having to attend an autopsy, even visiting the morgue was one part of the job Montrose hated. He always puked afterwards and it was embarrassing. It was the smell that did it. Montrose couldn't cope with it. Nor everything else that went with the procedure.

Fielding thought it all a joke. Not how the victim had died, but his boss's aversion to dead bodies being opened up and probed about in. 'It never bothers me,' he told Montrose at their first autopsy together. 'I'm a butcher's son and was brought up with the smell of blood and my father's cotton apron covered in it. Medical examiners and butchers do the same job, you know. They cut up carcasses and take the insides out.'

Montrose had thrown up there and then and Fielding had never let him live it down. They worked well together though, and Fielding was loyal. Montrose knew he could depend on his sergeant so he allowed him his fun without a reprimand.

'The killer used the victim's scarf, very convenient if you think about it. The woman's medical records show she was diagnosed with colon cancer in March, which corresponds with my findings. Late-stage so any treatment would have been futile. Strangulation isn't a nice death but at least it's fairly quick. It saved her a good deal of pain to come, actually,' the pathologist told them.

'That's helpful,' Montrose replied sarcastically. Martin Jones was good at his job, an expert, but Montrose found his flippancy somewhat inappropriate.

'I do my best,' Martin said amused. Julie Merriton's body lay on a post mortem autopsy table. The white sheet covering her had been pulled down to expose her face, neck, shoulders and chest. A wide V shape of stitches showed Martin's incisions. 'Anyway, there isn't anything more I can tell you, except the time of death. That will be in my detailed report which I'll have winged over to you tomorrow morning.

'Can you give me a ballpark figure for the time of death?' Montrose asked, starting to feel queasy.

'I would say ten pm, or thereabouts. Are you all right, DCI Montrose, you look a little pale.'

Montrose made it out into the corridor. He took deep breaths and walked as quickly as his shaky legs and heaving stomach would take him. Outside, he leaned against the police car and tried to focus on a building in the distance. He'd heard it helps with nausea or was it only seasickness. Fielding joined him after a few minutes.

'Well done, Sir,' he said, patting Montrose on the back.

'Take your hands off me, and less of it, sergeant.' Montrose glared back at Fielding, letting the man know he'd had enough of the jibes for one day.

DCI Peter Montrose drove to Woodbury eager to be home. After a day at work, all Peter wanted to do was have a shower, put on his civvies, as he liked to call them, and go downstairs for a glass of his favourite tipple, whisky with a splash of soda. Tonight he walked along the path with the thought of a drink uppermost in his mind. Well, that and Julie Merriton's murder.

When he parked his car on the driveway of Primrose Cottage and saw Jake's motorbike, his expression changed. He liked Jake but because of his attachment to Amelia's sister, Grace, he visited often, and this week it had been four evenings in a row. Montrose felt put out by it. He longed to spend some quality time alone with Amelia. Any discussion they started concerning their upcoming wedding, Grace voiced her opinion on what kind of cake, flowers, colours and the style of dresses the bridesmaids should wear. Jake joined in when he was there and Peter was getting tired of it. Amelia knew his views on how their wedding should be and so she took her sister's well-meaning advice in her stride. She ignored most of it and carried on with the plans already decided on. Often Amelia would give him a look as if to say, 'they mean well.'

He had never regretted giving up his rented house in Hoole to move in with Amelia, six months ago. It was what he wanted. To be with the woman he had fallen deeply in love with when they'd first met eighteen months ago. Even though his journey to work took an extra thirty minutes, he didn't mind. He enjoyed the solitude of his car and his choice of music, a background of melody playing low so it wouldn't intrude on his thoughts.

The evening was warm and the cottage windows were open wide. The aroma of spices and curry wafted towards him cheering him a little. Peter painted on a smile and walked into the kitchen. Amelia had been chopping onions, her eyes still red and watering. She came to him for a hug.

'Hi, how was your day, I missed you,' she said after she had kissed him lightly on the lips.

'Hi, what about your day, I missed you too.'

It was a habitual exchange of greeting, a joke between the two of them. Neither of them bothered to go into detail about the day they had just spent, they didn't need to. Amelia understood Peter's reluctance to talk about police work and she knew he had little interest in the pattern of a fabric or the colour of paint she was using for a particular client. It was enough that they had asked, knowing that if there was something important that needed saying, it would be. Today was one of those days.

'I need to speak to you later, it's important, Amelia.' Peter whispered in her ear before pulling away.

Amelia nodded and turned to Grace. 'Will you and Jake find something to do this evening instead of staying in? Peter and I want some alone time. It's a beautiful evening and a shame to waste it.'

'Good idea,' Jake agreed.

Peter looked at Amelia in amazement. If he'd known it would be that easy, he would have suggested it long before now.

Amelia's home cooking made his mouth water and he always looked forward to the evening meal she had prepared for the three of them. Four when Jake was visiting.

After they had finished eating and Grace and Jake had gone out, Amelia and Peter had gone to bed and spent an hour in each other's arms making up for the lost time. After their lovemaking they sat together side by side snuggled up, the duvet pulled up to their waists with a glass of cooled chardonnay in their hand.

'Come on then, tell me what's troubling you,' Amelia asked, after taking a sip.

'How well do you know Vivien Anderson?'

'Quite well and I like her.' Amelia thought she might know where this was leading and readied herself.

'She visited you recently, you said, when she returned from Rome?'

'Yes, it was just after Mark's funeral.'

'You told me she was very upset. Was it just about Mark's death, or was there something else bothering her?'

'She seemed more distracted than upset but that's to be expected, considering the circumstances, why?'

'I don't usually make a habit of divulging confidential information to you regarding any of my cases, Amelia.

Unfortunately, the one I'm working on at the moment involves people we know and I think I may need your help.' Montrose finished his drink and put the glass back on the bedside table.

'What can I do?'

'A middle-aged woman was found strangled in Grosvenor Park recently, and I think Mark may have been having an affair with the victim. They have a history from twenty-odd years ago and they may have rekindled their relationship.'

Amelia knew instantly that Peter was barking up the wrong tree if he thought Vivien had found out about the affair and it was causing her distress. She didn't want to be disloyal to Vivien so she stayed silent but knew she was going to have to tell Peter sooner rather than later what her friend had confided.

'I had reason to question Vivien about it and although her answers were plausible my gut feeling is that she's holding something back. I had the impression she was afraid, and certainly very nervous. I remember you telling me that she confides in you. Did she confide in you about anything to do with Mark that day?'

'She has in the past, generally concerning how trapped she feels being married to him. Honestly, Peter, you wouldn't believe some of the things she told me about him? I would have left him years ago, and I encouraged her to do just that. She wouldn't because of how it would affect her daughter, and yet, Isobel has no respect for her mother, Grace can confirm that.'

Peter pulled Amelia towards him and kissed her. 'So she mentioned nothing about her time in Rome?' he asked, after releasing her from his hold.

Amelia sipped her chardonnay. The silence was noted by the ticking of an alarm clock by her side. Eventually, after thinking it through and the consequences if she stayed silent, she said, 'Vivien did tell me something,

Peter, but I promised not to mention it to you.'

'Do you intend to keep that promise?'

'Not if you ask me nicely.' Amelia smiled leaning on Peter's shoulder. He responded and kissed her again, long and hard.

'Is that nice enough?' he asked. Amelia smiled at him.

'So, what did she say, my love?'

'She told me that Antonio Cortez, the man who befriended Isobel and Grace in Rome and is staying at Lilac House, had a business deal with Mark involving a stolen painting. A painting attributed to Caravaggio.' Amelia didn't think it necessary at this stage to tell Peter Vivien had the stolen painting.

'Is that all, did she mentioned how Mark planned to pay for the painting?'

'I think she mentioned something about uncut diamonds.'

'You will tell me if you remember anything else she said, won't you?'

'Of course, I will.' Amelia snuggled down under the covers ready to call it a night.

Disappointed and somewhat disgruntled, Montrose said goodnight and turned over onto his side away from his fiancé. There was more to this, and he knew that not only was Vivien hiding something from him, but his fiancé was too.

CHAPTER 26

Vivien

The shock of Julie Merriton's death has left me even more stressed and anxious for Isobel. I suspect Antonio may have had something to do with it, but because he was with Isobel, I can't see how it's likely. I miss Amelia and the excitement of helping her with the wedding arrangements. Ever since I confided in her I've regretted it. She will always think of me as a thief, and perhaps never trust me again.

This morning I received two letters. One from Gerrard and Gafferty our solicitors, informing me of the contents of Marks will. I already knew what was in his will. Everything we owned together we put in joint names so it came as no surprise that Mark has left everything to me. To be precise he's left half of everything to me because I already own the other half. Everything except the numerous shares and two bank accounts he had that I knew nothing about. The money from these he has left to Isobel. The documents in question have been passed on to the probate office, and we will hear from our solicitors shortly.

Mark had taken out insurance that will clear the mortgage on the house and I'm grateful for that, at least. All I have to worry about now is the mortgage repayments on the barn conversion we had done to accommodate the business so that Anderson Antiques can continue. This is the incentive I need to stop procrastinating and get the business up and running again.

The second letter is from Jack Tyler. I had given up hope of ever hearing from him again but here he is asking if he can visit me the day after tomorrow. The printed heading at the top of the sheet of paper, reads, Custom and Excise, with the address of his office in Manchester, so I assume it is not going to be a social call. I am to text my consent and he has scribbled his mobile number under his signature. I'm undecided what I should do.

Isobel and Antonio have taken my car again and they went out early so I haven't seen them this morning. I assume they are doing more sightseeing. They visited Chirk Castle yesterday, so goodness knows where they will end up today. I tucked Jack's letter into my pocket and walked the short distance to the barn. I was shocked to find the office door unlocked and then remembered I had opened it when looking for wrapping paper and string to wrap up the paintings I'd stored in Mark's Mercedes. Everywhere and every item in the barn needed to be dusted and the carpets vacuumed, and I made a mental note.

Before locking the door to the office and barn I decided to answer Jack's letter. I sent him a text and told him it will be fine for him to visit when suggested, and asked him to confirm what time he would be arriving. Now that was done and off my mind, I relaxed a little and returned to the house to begin preparing lunch. I must have been preoccupied with the thought of seeing Jack again that I didn't notice my car parked on the driveway. Imagine my shock when I walked into the kitchen and saw Antonio reading the letter I'd received from the solicitors. Thankfully Jack's letter lay in its envelope back in the office.

'Excuse me. That letter is private.' I took it out of Antonio's hand berating myself for leaving it for him to find. Antonio's self-satisfied expression made me want to punch him.

'Very interesting,' he replied, and then added quietly so Isobel wouldn't hear. 'You only have three more days left.'

Fuming, I began to prepare lunch for the three of us. I needed to get Isobel away from Antonio for a while so I asked her if she would accompany me to the local supermarket for the groceries we needed. We hadn't spent any time together since her return from Italy and that was down to Antonio taking up most of it. Not that Isobel was complaining. Antonio can search the rest of the house while we're out, I thought, having lost the will to care anymore. He was leaning against the worktop with his arms folded watching me. 'Antonio won't mind, will you?' I said.'

'I need to make a few telephone calls so I'll do that while you're both out. Is it okay for me to use your landline, Vivien? The reception on my mobile isn't good.'

I gladly agreed even though I knew the calls were probably to Italy and would heighten my telephone bill.

Our local supermarket has a cafeteria and Isobel and I stopped for a coffee while we were there. Although we did need food and other household items, my real reason for getting Isobel alone was for a different matter. While we waited for our drinks I began the conversation. 'Where did you go for dinner last night, anywhere nice?'

'We went to Hanky Panky Pancakes. Grace told me about it, so I thought we'd give them a try.' Isobel paused while a waitress offloaded the drinks onto our table.

'Was the food good?'

'Very good, yes,' Isobel said.

'So what was the film like, did it meet your expectations?'

'It did, but I don't think Antonio was impressed. He was restless the whole time we were in the cinema.'

'Where did you both spend the night?'

'The Travelodge, I told you. I watched a programme on the television in our room and had room service bring me up a gin and tonic. Happy days,' Isobel laughed.

'Where was Antonio, wasn't he with you?' This was the question foremost on my mind.

'Well, funny you should ask. After we booked into the hotel, he wanted to go outside for a cigarette. He told me later that he'd arranged to meet someone. They had met, he said, in Italy a few months ago and this person by coincidence now lived in Chester. He was apologetic for not telling me earlier but I was a bit miffed, to be honest.'

I knew exactly who Antonio had arranged to meet, and what he'd done. It made me shudder. The thought of my daughter in the company of a murderer was terrifying.

'Was he out long? Not very nice of him to leave you on your own,' I managed to say calmly.

'That's what I thought. He left around nine-thirty, probably only out for an hour, but even so. So much for a nice romantic night away together, eh Mum? Oh! By the way, I should have mentioned it earlier. Your bank telephoned and asked to speak to you. They knew Dad had passed away and said they need to speak to you urgently. It's something about payment on a loan?'

The telephone call from the bank was unexpected. A loan I knew nothing about, but was expected to pay off, worried me. 'I'll telephone them later,' I told Isobel distractedly.

I sat thinking about what Isobel had just told me about Antonio. Peter had asked me to let him know if I thought of, or found out, anything which would help with his inquiry into the death of Julie Merriton. The last thing I wanted was for Isobel to be drawn into his investigation. She was an innocent victim of Antonio's manipulation and I thought the less she knew the better.

On the day of Jack's visit, Isobel and Antonio had once again gone out on one of their jaunts. Antonio was due to fly home the following day and I knew he would approach me later for the money he thought I owed him. I looked forward to Jack's visit even if it was going to be all business and no pleasure. I desperately needed his help, and to get it I knew my only option was to own up and give him back the painting.

Unexpectantly David arrived half an hour before Jack was due to arrive. He'd taken Mark's Mercedes out for a test drive the day before so I guessed it was to return the car keys to me. Before I had the chance to say I was expecting a visitor, he brought out his iPad and began showing me photos of the exact make and model and the retail price. He then made me a reasonable offer which I refused.

'I'm not ready to sell it just yet.' I told him.

Before we could discuss it further, Jack arrived, and to my utter surprise, the two men shook hands like old friends. I suddenly recalled the time in the Vatican when I'd come across them both deep in conversation. At the time I had presumed they were discussing the stunning architecture or one of the numerous old masters on display. I'd had an impression then that they were more than polite strangers.

'You know each other,' I said. Not a question.

David looked embarrassed when Jack replied. 'Yes. Because of David's frequent visits abroad, especially to the continent, we decided to recruit him. He is what we call, a freelance customs and excise undercover agent. He watches people for us; takes videos and sets up cameras, that sort of thing. He's helping us to collect evidence against the Cortez organisation.'

I was infuriated with both of them, fizzing with anger. I couldn't speak or respond, except to look at them both in disbelief.

'This summer in Rome was my first assignment, Viv, and I doubt I'll be doing anything like it again. Sorry, Jack.' Jack shrugged and made himself comfortable on one of the sofas. 'When Jack approached me and mentioned he had information concerning Alonzo Cortez and a dubious Caravaggio painting, and that it involved Mark, I was afraid you might get dragged into it. But let's face it; you did that willingly.'

'Were you watching me the whole time, then David?'

'Not all the time, mostly Antonio Cortez, and Mark.'

Had David also been on St Angelo's Bridge on the day of Mark's death, I wondered? Had he been following me that day and watched me exit Jack's hotel. I hadn't noticed him. I glared at David and turned to face Jack. 'Did your informer mention a Julie Merriton by any chance, Jack?' Jack looked back at me unblinking. It was unsettling. 'She initiated Mark into the arrangement she'd made with the Cortez family. Mark's passion for the painter Caravaggio was common knowledge, so she knew he would be an easy target. Did you know that Julie was found murdered the other night?'

'Yes,' Jack replied. David looked blank.

'How do you know that?' Jack asked, looking puzzled.

'Detective Chief Inspector Montrose visited to question me about Mark and Julie's relationship. He told me then.'

'What did you tell him?' Jack leaned towards me showing interest.

'That Mark and Julie had a short fling years ago

before Mark and I met. I told him Mark had taken a package of uncut diamonds to Rome for her, as a favour.'

'Did you mention Caplan and your involvement?' Jack asked.

'No, I didn't, should I have done?' I turned back to David. 'By the way, David, I did not willingly get involved in Mark's quest for a Caravaggio. I was left with little choice. If I remember rightly, you were the one that persuaded Mark to holiday in Rome in the first place, with your talk of Piazza Navona and Galleria Borghese. I thought it a strange choice at the time. The Canary Isles has always been his favourite place to holiday.' David looked embarrassed and his shifty glance at Jack confirmed my suspicions.

'I get it now. It was all part of your scheme, wasn't it, Jack? You used David in your cat and mouse game too, not just me. You're both partly responsible for Mark's death. In your effort to stop him delivering the diamonds, which one of you ran him down?'

'Now hold on a minute,' David expostulated.

'Why would I do that?' Jack asked. 'I wanted him to meet Caplan. That was the central part of the plan. It would have defeated the object to have him mowed down. Mark's accident was unfortunate, but just that, an accident.'

'So you say,' I snapped back. 'I would like you both to leave now. I have nothing further to say and I never want to see either of you again.' Shaking I walked to the door, opened it, and indicated for them to leave.

'This isn't a social call Vivien, but before I say anymore, is there something you'd like to tell me?' Jack led me back to the sofa. 'Sit down,' he demanded.

'No, I don't think so,' I said shrugging him away.

'Together we retrieved a holdall full of euros from the Rail Terminal locker, and Mark gave you the painting he'd thought he'd just paid for, to look after. Do you remember that?'

Vivien nodded. She knew where this was going.

'You stole that painting from my hotel room, didn't you? I purposely arranged it so that I sat next to you on the aeroplane, hoping you'd come clean and make your apology. Something along the lines of, sorry it was a spur of the moment thing. Yesterday, David and I found the missing painting in the boot of your husband's car. I now have a warrant for your arrest.'

'I was going to talk to you about that, Jack,' I said quietly, avoiding both men's eyes.

'Start talking now then,' Jack told me.

CHAPTER 27

The internal monologue that had been whirling in Vivien's brain since returning from Rome spilt out. She knew she couldn't avoid the truth of what she had done any longer. Her voice was clipped as she told Jack and David everything. Her visit to see Caplan and the key he'd given her. The attack on her way home and her handbag robbed. Then the key was stolen from her. Vivien looked at Jack at this point, but he ignored her silent plea for help. She went on to tell them she'd had another key cut to placate, Mark, and then Antonio. That she'd found Mark on the towpath after Antonio's men had left him there with terrible injuries, and finally, stealing the painting from Jack's hotel room.

'I thought once I came home everything would get back to normal. I did intend to give the painting back to you, Jack, or the Galleria. I just got carried away in the excitement of it all.'

Vivien carried on before either man could interrupt. That Isobel had insisted on going to Rome to see where her father had died. Finding out Antonio had befriended her daughter and then turning up on her doorstep. Antonio's threats, him wanting money she hadn't got, and how she only had until the following day to pay him. Mark borrowing half of the money for the painting from David and subsequently giving away a quarter of their business, and now the bank is insisting she pay instalments on a loan he had borrowed for the other half, or sell the house to pay off the debt. How she would have a nervous breakdown if Jack insisted on arresting her.

Jack listened to Vivien's explanation watching her unravel. He knew he was partly to blame for any breakdown she may have. He'd already known she was trapped in an unhappy and abusive marriage when he picked her up and put her in his car on the evening she was attacked. She'd been vulnerable and he had taken advantage of her. He didn't regret it, though. He hadn't been able to resist her. He'd seen the bruises just beginning to fade, as he had held her in his arms and smoothed her thick black hair away from her brow. Vivien had looked into his eyes, trusting and wanting. She was the sort of woman he had dreamed of meeting. The sort of woman he knew he could love, given a chance. Jack also knew that because of his actions he had blown away any likelihood of a lasting relationship with her. He'd had a job to do, and as much as he would have liked to have held her in his arms until morning, instead, he had taken the key and left. As always, his work took precedence.

Alonzo Cortez had eluded punishment by dying just as the net was beginning to tighten around him. Caplan and his associates had been rounded up and taken into custody. Jack's office, along with the Italian police had culminated enough evidence to proceed with prosecution but there was still Alonzo's son Antonio, to deal with.

What Vivien had just told them had given Jack food for thought. Without a doubt, Antonio had been sent to Cheshire with instructions to get rid of problems. Julie Merriton for one and Vivien could be another. What they needed was a confession from him.

David had listened to Vivien's explanation without comment but with concern on his face. He made coffee and topped up their mugs with a drop of whisky. He knew Vivien would need something to take the edge of her nerves. He needed it for the shock. Her actions were alien to him. All of a sudden she wasn't the fragile Vivien he knew, and something she'd said still bothered him. He passed Vivien her coffee.

'What were you doing in Jack's hotel room?' he questioned.

Exasperated that that was all David could think of in her moment of crisis, Vivien turned on him and somewhat sarcastically, replied, 'Having sex, what do you think?' The following silence was palpable. David left them without another word but the slamming of doors behind him explained how he felt.

Jack sat next to Vivien and took her hand in his. Vivien had held her tears back until then but with Jack's kind gesture, they began to flow. Jack held her in his arms until her sobbing ceased.

'It will be all right, Vivien. We can sort this.'

'How will it be alright if I'm in prison?'

Jack smiled down at her. 'I have a plan.'

Jack told Vivien what he proposed they should do. It was her decision, he told her. She could either help him bring Antonio to justice, or he would be obliged to arrest her for theft. It didn't take long for Vivien to decide, and she agreed to go along with his plan knowing it was the only way to put an end to the nightmare in which she was living.

As soon as Vivien managed to get a moment alone with Antonio she told him she had the money he wanted, and asked him to meet her that evening at nine pm in the barn.

The door to the barn had been unlocked earlier and Vivien switched on the light as she entered, grateful for the light. Around her, dark shadows filled every corner and the smell of beeswax from her polishing efforts wafted out into the night air. She turned on a small table lamp in the office and sat in a chair waiting for Antonio. She heard faint noises, and the occasional creak of wood, but knew it was the barn's old timbers beginning to settle for the night. The grandfather clock in the foyer chimed nine and almost immediately the outer door to the barn opened.

Antonio stood and looked around. When he saw Vivien he came into the office.

'Where is it?' he looked at Vivien in anticipation, apparently hoping to see a case or bag filled with his money.

'It's here, in the safe.' Vivien pointed to a medium-sized green metal safe in the corner of the room. 'Before I give you what you asked for there's something I must make clear, Antonio. This is a one-off payment. There won't be anymore.'

'I don't know about that.'

'What do you mean?'

'If anything happens to you, Vivien, Isobel inherits everything. I read Mark's will and the solicitor's letter remember.'

'Are you going to kill me too, liked you murdered Julie? I know it was you who did it, Antonio.'

'Get on with it, open the damn safe.'

'Please promise me you won't hurt Isobel,' Vivien begged.

'Isobel has nothing to do with this.'

'So your main purpose in coming to Chester was to deal with Julie Merriton?' To Vivien's horror Antonio pulled out a gun.

'No more questions,' Antonio commanded.

Vivien looked down the barrel of a small handgun and knew she'd gone too far.

Jack and DCI Montrose needed a confession and Jack had made it clear it was up to her to get one if she didn't want to spend time in prison. Vivien prayed she didn't get shot in the process and playing for time said, 'Is the painting Mark took from the locker at the Rail Terminal a fake? If so the uncut diamonds given to Caplan were for what?'

'What are you going on about now?'

'It was all a con, wasn't it? The paintings found in Castello Sforzesco were to be transported to Rome for authentication. That much is true, and they were. But someone, probably Caplan, put it about that a Caravaggio painting had been stolen by one of the curators before they could be taken to Rome. But that never happened, did it, Antonio? Caplan arranged for a fake Caravaggio painting to be placed in the locker for Mark to collect.' While Vivien talked she turned the dial for the combination code to open the safe and took out a bulky black plastic bag and placed it on the office desk. She stood with her hands resting on top, praying Antonio wouldn't want to open it just yet. 'Why did Julie have to die?' Vivien persisted. 'Was she a loose end? It won't matter if you tell me now. I couldn't go to the police, who would believe me?'

Antonio smiled. 'You think I work for Caplan? You don't know what you're talking about. Caplan is just a jeweller, a go-between. There is a fake Caravaggio painting, you're right in thinking that. I know because my father painted it. My father Alonzo Cortez was a talented artist. He arranged the deal, as he has done many times before. Unfortunately, he died before the deal could be completed. That means as head of the family, I'm now in charge.' He laughed at Vivien's surprised face and the self-satisfied look returned to his face. Antonio was impressed by Vivien's ability to work it out. She was correct in most of her assumptions but not all.

Antonio stood by the bag ready to look inside. He still felt a degree of anger towards his father. Sending

Matteo and Stefano to check on him had been humiliating. It proved Alonzo hadn't trusted his son to finish the job. Antonio was determined to do that now, even if it was only to prove his father wrong.

'Was Helena part of the plan?' As soon as the words were out of her mouth, Vivien could have kicked herself. Antonio raised his arm and levelled the gun at her.

'You don't have to do this,' Vivien cried out fearfully and to her relief, Antonio dropped his arm and the gun now rested beside his right leg. He heaved a sigh and sat down on the office chair.

'You ask about my sister. You should understand we all worked for our father in some way or another. Helena befriends lonely and vulnerable middle-aged wealthy men. They fall for her; she's beautiful, isn't she? A plan and a fake painting are already in place. These men not only covet a valuable painting but Helena also and in the process lose a good proportion of their money.'

'Mark fell for her, that's for sure.' Vivien thought about what Antonio had said earlier. 'What about Isobel?'

'The fling with Isobel means nothing. She provided a good reason and cover for me to come to Chester, that's all.'

'You mentioned that you would expect more money from me in the future, or from any inheritance Isobel will receive after my death. Well, let me put you clear on that if you're intending to blackmail. I only own three-quarters of the business and I have an enormous mortgage on the barn and a large loan set against the house that I'm struggling to pay.'

'I don't need anything from you or Isobel, now that I have this.' Antonio clutched the bag of money sitting in front of him on the table.

'You don't need to kill me either, do you?'

'My father was a large cog in an even larger wheel called Mafia. Do you understand, Vivien? I can't let you live and it's your fault, you shouldn't have interfered. You know too much and if I don't do it, someone, else will. I did kill Julie, you were right about that. She was a loose end, just like you.' Antonio stood and faced her. He raised the gun again. 'I'm sorry.'

Vivien shouted, HELP, as loud as she could and at the same time set off the pocket alarm Jack had given her earlier. Antonio fired and Vivien fell back, blood oozing from the wound.

Within seconds but too late, Jack Tyler and DCI Montrose came out of their hiding places from amongst the antique furniture. Antonio turned quickly and fired off two more shots in their direction. Jack Tyler fell to the floor as Montrose rushed forward and grappled with Antonio. The gun scuttled along the floor towards Vivien. She picked it up with her good arm and pointed it at Antonio, her whole body shaking.

Quickly handcuffed and with two large policemen on either side of him, Antonio looked diminished. He scowled at Vivien and shouted at her. 'You bitch, you set me up.'

Almost delirious with the burning pain in her shoulder, and relief, Vivien shouted back. 'Doesn't that make a change? Shoe's on the other foot now, isn't it, Antonio?'

Suddenly Isobel was there. She'd heard the ambulance and police car sirens and had rushed out of the house to see what was going on. She stood flabbergasted as she watched Sergeant Fielding manhandle Antonio into the back of the waiting police car. She looked at him through the car window questioningly. 'Antonio?' she called to him, but he turned his head away and ignored her.

Vivien sat down on the office chair waiting for her

racing heart to settle. Montrose left her and went to Jack who lay on the floor still inside the barn. One of the bullets had gone into Jack's thigh; the other bullet had skimmed his arm taking away a chunk of flesh. Montrose had administered a tourniquet to Jack's leg to help slow the flow of blood while Jack slipped in and out of consciousness. Montrose stayed with Jack while the paramedics lifted him and took him into a waiting ambulance and it seemed an age before the medics had finished attending to him. Eventually, the ambulance was ready to leave and drove off, sirens wailing, towards the Countess of Chester Hospital.

A second ambulance arrived soon after and paramedics gave preliminary attention to Vivien's wounds. She too was taken to hospital, leaving Isobel alone and tearful.

'I've asked Amelia and Grace to come over to keep you company,' Montrose told her. 'They'll stay the night if that's all right with you. They should be here soon. Will you be ok until then? I need to get back to the station.' Montrose gave Isobel a reassuring look before turning to leave. He carried away the black plastic bag. Not containing the money Antonio so desperately craved but cut up squares of newspaper about to be incinerated.

CHAPTER 28

Vivien

Isobel has secured a job within a building society in Chester. She seems happy and content in her new role. She's mentioned someone called Christopher on several occasions and when she does her face lights up. I'm hoping Christopher proves to be the balm Isobel needs to soothe her anguish over Antonio.

I wish I could conjure up a balm to soothe me. Jack hasn't been in touch since the night I was shot and returned from the hospital which is six weeks ago now. I thought at least he would check to see if I had recovered from my ordeal. I can't say I blame him though, considering my hare-brained actions and the mess I made of his investigation, but I'm sad nevertheless. I still hope that maybe he will get in touch again.

David and I are no longer friends, and there hasn't been an occasion where we might have cleared the air. I'm sad about that too. The longer the time goes on the more impossible it is for me to make the first move and telephone him. I still don't know what his intentions are regarding the business. I was hoping to discuss a few options at Amelia and Peter's wedding but regrettably, Amelia hasn't sent him an invitation. I recently learned from Isobel, through Grace, about David's underhanded behaviour when they first moved into the village and discovered the coffin. So considering their history I suppose it's no surprise.

After the wedding, which is in a few days, I'm

considering visiting Rome again. Not for a holiday this time, although I didn't have much of one last time I was there. I want to set matters straight with Detective Inspector Berardi, and I need to do it before I can move on with my life.

The church is full of wedding guests but Isobel and I manage to find a place at the end of a row. We slid along a pew and I sat beside the lady who runs the cake shop, Mrs Brownlow. She's wearing a large bright pink hat with a downward feather that ends inches from my face. I'm struggling to restrain myself from sneezing. David's sister Leonie is a few pews in front of us sitting with a person sporting a blonde afro hairdo.

Peter is stood at the front with his best man and they both look smart and handsome in their dark suits. Peter keeps turning towards the church door. He looks apprehensive as if he doubts Amelia will show up. Both men are tall and Peter's jacket fits him with only millilitres to spare. The best man is much slimmer than the groom and faces the front of the church. He leans heavily on a black walking stick and looks frail. I can't see his face but I think I may know him.

Suddenly the organ booms out the wedding march and everyone stands. Because Amelia has no father or uncle to give her away she decided Grace would have the honour. They walk down the aisle together hand in hand, Amelia in a long Ivory silk gown, Grace in mauve. Their grins and smiles say it all.

Peter and his best man have turned to watch them and for the first time, I catch a glimpse of the best man's face. Everyone sits and Peter and Amelia stand side by side ready for the wedding ceremony to begin.

I heard the vicar begin to speak but heard none of the words, just a faint mumbling in the background. Isobel nudged me and I straighten from my slump on the pew.

'Are you alright Mum?' she whispered.

I nod, but I wasn't alright. I wanted to cry because Peter's best man is Jack. He looks pale and ill, and a shadow of his former self.

The marque is dressed in fairy lights and flowers. The hired DJ plays a continuous melody of old and new hits, and the reception is in full swing. Amelia and Peter had the first dance and now the makeshift dance floor is full. A small bar serves alcohol and the guests' glasses are continually refilled. The buffet has been served, and the cake cut.

Isobel invited Christopher and they're sitting with Grace and Jake around a table near Jack who is alone. I'd just summoned up enough courage to go and speak to him when Amelia stopped me.

'Are you having a good time, Vivien? I am.'

'Yes and it's been a wonderful day,' I replied, smiling at Amelia who was a little tidily and giggling a lot.

'Doesn't Peter look handsome? I love him so much I could burst.' She turned to look at her new husband who was dancing with Mrs Brownlow, who thankfully had taken off her hat.

'Yes he does, so does the best man.'

'Oh Jack, yes. He and Peter have been friends since university days. Both studied law but they took off in different directions. Peter in the police force and Jack with the HM Customs and Excise. You know Jack, don't you?'

'Yes, we've met. I didn't realise he'd been ill.'

'He was shot by that Antonio fellow. Same night as you, didn't you know that?'

I looked from Amelia to Jack in dismay. 'Yes, but no one told me how badly he'd been injured.'

'He fared far worse than you. He took two bullets, one to his leg and the other took a chunk out of his upper arm. Luckily the bullet missed his femoral artery otherwise Peter would have been looking for another best man.'

I don't think Amelia meant to sound flippant but it irritated me nevertheless. 'Poor Jack,' I replied, sadly.

'Oh well, I'd better continue my mingling, see you later.' Amelia walked away, staggering a little.

I walked over to Jack and stood by the table. 'Hello, is it alright if I sit here for a moment?' I asked. His shoulders shrugged slightly as if he didn't care one way or the other and I took it as permission. 'I've only just been told about your ordeal. I would have visited you in the hospital if I had known.'

Jack took a mouthful of his drink. It was bottled water. 'It's okay. I was well out of it for a while anyway. I'm recovering slowly but I wanted to be here today for Peter and Amelia.'

'Are you in a lot of pain, still?' I asked when Jack winced as he turned in his chair to face me properly.

'Yeah, and probably will be for a long time yet. I'll be fine eventually, though. Once I've built my damaged muscles back up. I'm hoping to go back to work next week. I intended to get in touch you know, Vivien. Once I was back on my feet. I have something for you.'

'You did, you have,' I said flustered, feeling the comfort of Jack's words wash over me.

'Yes, it's back home in my apartment. Peter arranged for transport to get me here today. I'm unable to drive yet which is a nuisance. Did you come in your car, by any chance?'

'Yes why?'

'If you help me up, and drive, we can go now.' Jack leaned heavily on his stick and I put my arms around his waist and lifted him gently. Once standing I led the way out of the marquee towards where my car was parked.

Jack's apartment overlooked Chester Racecourse, known as the Roodee. It was spacious, minimalistic and a typical bachelor's pad, I thought. The view from the large window in the sitting room looked out over the racecourse and field. My father had been a keen racing enthusiast and I knew from him a little of the Roodee's history, It was recognised by the Guinness book of world records as the oldest racecourse still in operation. Horse racing at Chester dated back as early as the 16th century, with 1539 cited as the year it began. The racecourse lies on the banks of the River Dee and was the harbour for the roman settlement there.

Daylight was fading fast and street lights were coming on all over the city but towards the centre of the field, I could see a mound and just make out a small cross on top of it. 'What's that over there?' I asked, pointing my finger. Jack was busy making coffee and he left the kitchen area to join me by the window.

'It's known as a rood. The racecourse name originates from it, Rood by the River Dee – Roodee.'

'Yes, I think I've heard of that before but why is it there?' I persisted.

Jack walked back to the kitchen and returned with my coffee. He handed it to me and I took a sip.

'You've put whisky in this.'

'Yes, I know.' We stood together looking out of the window. After a few minutes, Jack said, 'According to legend, the cross marks the burial site of the Virgin Mary. She was supposed to hang after causing the death of Lady Trawst, the wife of the Governor of Hawarden.'

'You're making this up?' I said incredulously. Jack shook his head and he chuckled. I didn't know what to think.

'The legend states that Lady Trawst had gone to church to pray for rain. Her prayers were answered by a thunderous storm and the statue was loosened and fell, killing her.'

'Oh, a statue of the Virgin Mary,' I said, the penny suddenly dropping. 'Go on.'

'Lady Trawst's husband couldn't stand to look at the statue afterwards and wanted it removed from the church. As a holy object hanging or burning the statue would be sacrilege so the Virgin Mary statue was carried down to the river in Hawarden and left on the bank. An unusually high tide carried it down from Hawarden to Chester, where she was put on trial and found guilty by twelve men, the jury, and buried over there.'

'I still think you're making it up,' I said.

'There's an alternative version.'

'I thought there might be.'

'The statue was instead carried from the bank here in Chester and taken to St. John's church. An ancient statue of the Virgin Mary was recorded there at the time of the reformation. It was thrown down as a relic of popery. So it's still likely the statue is out there under the mound.' Jack walked back to the kitchen for his coffee and then sat on one of the chairs around the dining table. 'Aren't you more interested in what I have for you?' he asked.

'Yes, what is it?' I replied.

'It's on my bed.' Jack pointed to a door leading off from the sitting room. It led back into his small hallway. 'Second door on the right, he called, as I left the room.

In Jack's bedroom, I stood mesmerised. Not by the decor, or the large bed, or the beautiful art deco lamp on his bedside table. It was what was on the bed that had me stunned. The painting 'Boy Peeling Fruit' held my gaze. I sensed Jack standing behind me.

'It's yours if you still want it,' he said, slipping his arms around my waist and pulling me back towards him.

He nuzzled my neck and kissed me beside my ear. I could feel myself beginning to melt into him but I undid his hands and moved away. I wasn't about to let him mess with my head again.

'What's going on Jack?'

'I don't know what you mean,' he replied, looking all innocent.

'Yes, you do. Why have you still got the painting?'

'It's complicated.'

'It always is with you isn't it.'

'You've got room to talk.'

'Well?'

Jack sighed and walked back into his sitting-room. I took one last look at the painting and followed him.

'When I returned from Rome, my boss was impatient and breathing down my neck for the results of my investigation. Things were coming to a head and he'd already arranged for the art expert to view the painting the following day. The painting you had taken and I no longer had. I told him, for security reasons, I'd decided to mail it to my office in Manchester from Rome, and was waiting for it to arrive. I hoped you'd see sense and return it to me. So I bided my time waiting for you to do the right thing. I wasn't completely sure it still existed. You could have destroyed it for all I knew. I don't mean intentionally, but it's easily done. Or maybe you'd sold it, or had given it to Antonio to get him off your back.'

'You know I would never do that.'

'No, I didn't know, Vivien. Anyway, when I eventually made out my report I only listed the euros we recovered from the locker.'

'If I had returned the painting to you, how would you have explained it to your boss, it suddenly turning up?'

'I would have crossed that bridge when I came to it. Then David and I found the painting in Mark's car but by then it was too late to do anything about it. It's been recorded as lost in the Italian postal system. Besides, the Italian art expert Berardi commissioned confirmed that all the paintings in Alonzo Cortez's studio and Antonio's apartment, are fake. This one is too, and so worthless. I thought it might be worth something to you though, Vivien. I know how much you like it.'

'So legally, I can keep it. You're not going to come back and arrest me for having it are you, like you threatened?'

'I'm sorry about that.'

'You did it to frighten me into doing your dirty work.'

'I didn't know Antonio would arrive armed, I'd never deliberately put you in danger.'

'I don't believe that for one minute. You blackmailed me with the threat of prison to make me go along with your plan to get a confession out of Antonio. I could have been killed. Antonio was already under suspicion for murdering Julie Merriton so you knew he was dangerous but it didn't stop you from using me as bait. Mark put me in danger when he sent me to Caplan with a bag of valuable diamonds. He didn't care what happened to me either, as long as he got his Caravaggio. You're no better than Mark. Am I so dispensable? What was it you called me, a mule.'

'I'm sorry, Vivien. Let me make it up to you. Take the painting, please.'

I couldn't look at Jack at that moment. I thought of all he had put me through, and his threat of an arrest and prison if I didn't comply with his plan. Since that night I'd lived on tenterhooks, waiting for the police to arrive any minute to question me. I hadn't been able to sleep and apart from the pain, I still had flashbacks and nightmares, reliving that evening on a continual spin. Admittedly Jack was ill in hospital but surely he could have gotten word to me somehow. Peter Montrose had telephoned once concerning Antonio's arrest but hadn't divulged enough to put my mind at rest. I knew I was partly responsible for a lot of the anxiety I felt. I wasn't blameless but knowing that didn't help. I felt alone and let down.

'Stuff the painting, I don't want it.' I said. I picked up my handbag and walked out of his apartment.

CHAPTER 29

I'm back in Rome and staying at the Caravaggio, the hotel Jack and I stayed in the first night we spent together. I don't have the same room but the layout and furniture are almost identical. I have an appointment tomorrow to see Detective Inspector Berardi. There is so much I need to get off my chest.

Since the evening of Amelia and Peter's wedding, I've had numerous texts and messages left on my answering machine from Jack asking me to get in touch. One text confirmed that the payment of euro's we retrieved from the locker, and now held with the custom and excise, are legally mine and will be returned to me in due course. It means I can pay David off, and regain full control of Anderson Antiques. I'm so relieved. Jack wants to meet up, to talk, to explain, although I've no idea what he could say that I don't already know. I've agreed and we are to have dinner the evening I return from my weekend in Rome. Maybe my future happiness isn't wrecked after all.

Detective Inspector Berardi looks the same and wearing his usual choice of clothing, expertly pressed. There are shadows under his eyes now that weren't there before. Did I contribute to those I wonder as I take a seat in his small tidy office?

'Mrs Anderson, it is a pleasure to see you again. How are you?' he shakes my hand in both of his.

'Hello Detective Inspector, thank you for agreeing to

see me.'

'Is this a social visit just to say hello, or do you have something else on your mind.' He smiled at me knowingly and I almost lost my nerve.

'I'm here to confess,' I said. 'It's my fault my husband is dead.' Berardi looked at me steadily. He didn't seem shocked or surprised.

'Suppose you tell me what happened.' He said, leaning back in his chair.

'I lied to you Inspector. I was on the towpath the day Mark died.'

'Go on.'

'As I crossed the bridge I saw two men who I'd previously seen with Antonio Cortez, come up the steps from under St Angelo's bridge. After they left I went down and found Mark.'

Berardi nodded and I thought he was about to say something. I waited but he just sat looking at me.

'He'd been very badly beaten and was laying on the very edge of the path. I knew if he turned over he would fall into the river. I should have tried to move him but he demanded I go for help, so I did.'

'Did your help take the form of an anonymous phone call to the Polizia? Mrs Anderson.'

'Yes, I'm sorry. I should have gone back and tried to move him, and I feel very guilty that I didn't. So you see, he must have rolled over into the water and drowned. It's my fault he's dead.'

'Or maybe he was helped. Perhaps he didn't roll over but was pushed into the River Tiber. All it would have taken was a little push.'

I met the weariness in Berardi's eyes. 'Do you think that was what happened? Someone pushed Mark into the River.'

'We'll never know, will we? The case is now closed, the verdict confirmed, accidental death by drowning. By the way, the lipstick, it was yours wasn't it?'

'Yes, it must have fallen out of my pocket when I knelt beside Mark.'

'Customs and Excise recovered the stolen Caravaggio painting I mentioned to you.'

'Oh good, that was a result then.' I replied.

'No, regrettably it was stolen again. Seems it just disappeared into thin air. I don't suppose you know anything about that? No, of course, you don't.' I sensed a note of sarcasm in the policeman's voice.

'It was a forgery though, wasn't it?'

'Actually, the painting in question is an authentic early version of Caravaggio's Boy Peeling Fruit. The copy Alonzo Cortez painted, destined for your husband was still in his studio when we searched his house. Seems there was a mix-up and the genuine Caravaggio ended up in the rail terminal locker, instead of the fake.' Berardi stood and held out his hand for me to shake. The meeting was at an end, I was being dismissed. 'Goodbye Mrs Anderson and take care.'

I placed my hand in the Inspector's and he gave it a slight shake but didn't let go. As soon as his grip loosened I quickly slipped my hand from his. 'Goodbye Inspector.'

On the flight back to Manchester I relaxed into my seat and closed my eyes and went over the conversation I'd had with Berardi. The painting Jack had and had offered to me was the genuine article. The exchange of diamonds and the purchase of a genuine Caravaggio painting was all part of a confidence trick. Mark was meant to receive a fake Boy Peeling Fruit, painted by Alonzo Cortez. Everything had gone wrong, or right, whichever way you wanted to look at it.

The policeman's words came back to me. 'All it

would have taken was a little push.'

His voice sounded loud in my ears and I thought for a moment he was there on the aeroplane. I opened my eyes. An attractive air hostess was serving drinks to a couple sitting in the seats in front of me. The man was saying, 'Just a little ice in my whisky.'

I relaxed again and the drone of the engine lulled me. I felt at peace and excited all at once. I would meet Jack and forgive him and say yes, I would like the painting after all. I knew my life would be different from now on, better. No more bruises to try and hide. No more walking on eggshells and worrying in case I said the wrong thing. No more dreading bedtime and having to zone out and find a happy place to hide in. I looked out of the small oval window and smiled. Berardi will never know how close to the truth he came.

When I stood looking down at Mark lying crushed and helpless on the towpath I felt sorry for him. Then as I stood listening to him berating me and his threat to make me suffer, a change came over me. I bent down and looked into his face and though it was swollen and smeared with blood I looked into his eyes hoping to see a glimmer of something. Not love, I never expected that. Perhaps a flicker of the man I'd fallen in love with all those years ago. I saw only hatred and loathing and my pity for him vanished.

I decided there and then that I wasn't going to let Mark hurt me anymore. So I held out my arms and placed them on Mark and just a little push was all it took.

The End

The mystery of Caravaggio's death solved at last – painting killed him.

In 2010, Tom Kington from The Guardian newspaper wrote an article with the above title. He then went on to explain:

Scientists seeking to shed light on the mysterious death of the Italian artist in 1610 said they are "85% sure" they have found his bones thanks to carbon dating and DNA checks on remains excavated in Tuscany.

Caravaggio's suspected bones come complete with levels of lead high enough to have driven the painter mad and helped finish him off.

"The lead likely came from his paints – he was known to be extremely messy with them," said Silvano Vinceti, the researcher who announced the findings today.

"Lead poisoning won't kill you on its own – we believe he had infected wounds and sunstroke too – but it was one of the causes."

Art historians already suspect that Goya and Van Gogh may have suffered from the ill effects of the lead in their paints, which can cause depression, pain and personality changes.

https://www.theguardian.com/artanddesign/2010/jun/16/caravaggio-italy-remains-ravenna-art

ACKNOWLEDGEMENTS

Eternal thanks to my daughters Joanne Phillips and Dawn Hamilton for their support, encouragement and enthusiasm to write my second book. Thanks to my patient friends and their frequent question, 'Have you finished it yet?' which gave me the motivation I needed.

Thanks to author Joanne Phillips for her help in getting my book published and the wonderful design of the book's cover.

Thanks to Dawn Hamilton, my proof-reader, for reading my manuscript multiple times and commenting.

Many thanks to the Wikipedia website for allowing me to use a copy photograph of Caravaggio's painting: Boy Peeling Fruit.

I relied on Google for research along with Helen Langdon's, Caravaggio: A Life. Caravaggio Painter of Miracles by Francine Prose, and Peter Watson and Cecilia Todeschini's, The Medici Conspiracy.